A Shift in Fortune

Lost Legacies Book 3

Maddox Grey

GREYMALKIN

Cover Design by Seventhstar Art

eBook ISBN: 978-1-7375381-7-2
Paperback ISBN: 978-1-7375381-9-6

The Lost Legacies Series

A Shift in Darkness*

A Shift in Shadows

A Shift in Fate

A Shift in Fortune

A Shift in Ashes

A Shift in Wings

A Shift in Death

A Shift in Tides

*A Shift in Darkness is available for free download at
maddoxgreyauthor.com.

To Clio and Dahlia. My dynamic duo forever.

Also to the person who kept sending me increasingly rude messages about my books having too many queer characters. Enjoy this sapphic romance.

xoxo.

Chapter One

A LOUD WHINE followed by a grinding sound caused me to jolt upright. My golden wings had gotten tangled in the sheets while I slept, and I frantically tried to get free of them while whatever was making that sound hit a new high pitched level.

"Get off!" I snarled. The light cotton sheets ripped in my hands. The racket died and I sat their panting with the torn sheets in my hands, wings drooping behind me. "Coffee grinder," I muttered.

Those hadn't been a thing in Tír na mBeo, the fae realm I'd grown up in, because *coffee* hadn't been a thing. But everyone here loved their coffee, and I had to admit even I was acquiring a taste for it. It was most likely Elisa or Magos in the kitchen; they both seemed determined to feed me constantly. I was also secretly convinced that vampires actually sustained themselves on caffeine and not blood.

I glanced at the digital clock next to my bed. Just past noon. That would make it lunch then. My feathers ruffled against each other as I rose from the bed. Some days I still woke in the early morning, but I was getting used to waking in the afternoon and staying up until the early hours of the morning like everyone else.

Coffee grinders. Different schedule. New home. Everything in my life felt like it was something new for me to get used to. Even my damn hair had changed from a dark brown to a rich auburn.

I ambled over to the chest to find something to wear as I tried to center myself. Grabbing a plain black t-shirt, I yanked it out only for it to snag on a loose nail and rip as I pulled it free. *Damn it.* I also had a lovely new amount of strength to deal with. I'd always had a strong build. Some of it was natural, and some of it was from moving around heavy barrels and supplies in the fae tavern I'd worked at for the last few years. But now it was on a whole other level.

This was third piece of clothing I'd torn in the last week, not counting the sheets I'd wrecked this morning. Nemain and her friends had bought all this for me because I didn't have any money. I tucked the torn shirt underneath all the other ones and grabbed a new one. With slow, deliberate movements I shut the drawer.

My adoptive fae parents had always described me as steady and dependable. They'd never asked anything of me growing up, but I still felt like I owed them something after they took me in when I was abandoned in their village. Not every fae family would have adopted a random non-fae baby and treated her so well. I'd wanted to make them proud, and I'd always been the type of person who needed a purpose. Back then, my purpose had been supporting my fae parents and our small town by doing supply runs and other odd jobs. Now I had a new purpose. Protect Finn.

My ever so helpful mind served up the memory of Finn struggling against a fae warrior while I screamed, unable to help him. I had failed him then, and if Nemain hadn't been there to save us, I don't know what would have happened.

The handle of the drawer snapped in my hand.

"Our Bryn is steady as a rock, she is." The words of my adoptive mother Faye played in my head. Rubbing my forehead, I tossed the broken handle on top of the dresser. I missed Faye and her partner Aldric so much.

They knew I was safe, but I'd only spoken to them once since coming to the human realm. Aldric told me they were proud of me, and Faye asked if I was getting enough to eat. As soon as they'd faded from the mirror I'd used to contact them, I'd excused myself and retreated to my room where I'd promptly burst into tears. That was the first and last time I'd let myself fall apart. Finn needed me to be strong, and I would be for him. Not only because we were bonded for life but because I loved him like a little brother.

My magic stirred, feeling like a leviathan rising from the ocean depths. I concentrated on my breathing as I braided my dark auburn hair, lulling my magic back to sleep. These past couple months, I'd been practicing my fighting skills but had done little with my magic. Despite being surrounded by others who possessed extraordinary magic, none of them had valkyrie magic and they understood little of it. Nemain promised me she was working on finding a proper mentor, but I worried we were running out of time. I didn't know what would happen if my magic rose and I wasn't able to pull it back. I'd expressed my concerns to Nemain, but she'd just shrugged and said, "Eh. We'll likely survive. I suppose if you destroy this building we'll have to hide from Pele for a bit since I promised her the lot of you were house-trained."

Feeling as centered as I was likely to get, I finished getting dressed and wrapped my wings around myself like a cloak.

"Good morning," Elisa said cheerfully, despite it being the afternoon.

The smell of bacon floated over to me, and I almost drooled. Magos was sitting on the couch reading a book. Finn was lying on the living room floor, coloring something on a notepad. He kept glancing up at Magos curiously before darting his eyes back to his drawing.

"Nemain and Mikhail at it again?" I slipped onto one of the kitchen stools and picked up the coffee Elisa had set down for me.

The dynamics of this group were odd, and I was still trying to figure them out. Nemain and Mikhail were the most confusing of all. They constantly fought with each other, but at the same time, there was clearly trust and a connection between them. It'd only gotten worse since Andrei, Nemain's werewolf lover, had left town for good. I'd walked into the third-floor apartment yesterday that Nemain, Magos, and Mikhail shared, just in time to see Nemain throw one of the kitchen stools at Mikhail's head. He'd turned into mist to dodge it, and the stool had smashed against the wall. Then they'd argued over whose fault it was that the stool was scattered in multiple pieces across the living room.

I didn't blame Magos at all for coming to our floor to escape their bickering.

"Yes," Magos said with a grimace. He rose from the couch and joined us in the kitchen, pouring himself a cup of coffee. "I forbade them from using any weapons on each other because I don't want to clean up all the blood splatters. When I left, Mikhail had Nemain in a headlock and was telling her to 'say uncle'." Magos made air quotes. "I'm pretty sure Nemain was seconds away from passing out."

Elisa chuckled. "Between them upstairs and Isabeau downstairs, this floor is the only peaceful place in the building." She placed a stack of blueberry pancakes on the kitchen island, along with a plate full of bacon. I jumped up and grabbed some plates from the cupboard and some silverware. Elisa placed a couple of smaller pancakes on a plate and paused by the bacon. "Finn, do you want any bacon?"

"No, thank you," he said.

Elisa plopped the plate down next to him and playfully ruffled his hair. "That's a nice drawing. We'll have to ask Nemain if she can pick up more drawing pads for you." Finn's odd green and yellow eyes fixed on her, and he nodded slowly and nibbled on a pancake.

"How is Isabeau handling the lockdown?" I asked when Elisa slid onto the stool between me and Magos.

Her arm brushed against my wing, and I worked hard to keep my features even. I had developed a ridiculous crush on the dark-haired vampire almost immediately, but I wasn't sure if she felt the same. Elisa was nice to everyone. I thought she had flirted with me before, but now I wasn't sure, and I didn't want to make things awkward. Plus, my flirting skills weren't great. The fae girl I'd been dating for a while had teased me mercilessly about how little game I had. Gods, it would be so embarrassing if I tried to flirt with Elisa only to find out she thought of me only as a friend.

"Isabeau"—Elisa slurped some coffee—"is a terror. I know why Nemain has wanted us all to stay inside the last couple of months, but if we don't get Isabeau out of this building for a few hours, she might smother us all in our sleep."

"I'll talk to her about it," Magos said. "She's been a little on edge lately as she processes her new . . . situation."

Guilt nipped at me. Nemain had agreed to join and serve the Unseelie Court. In exchange, the fae queens would keep their claws off Finn for fifty years and not subject him to court politics. I gladly would have offered myself instead, but the Unseelie Queen had her eyes on Nemain and was all too keen to use the situation to her advantage. Nemain didn't blame me, but I still considered myself responsible for the whole thing. If I'd done a better job of protecting Finn, Nemain wouldn't have had to give up so much. The conversation turned to lighter topics as we continued to munch on our breakfasts, until the door to the third-floor apartment opened and slammed shut. We all paused and stared at the front door in anticipation.

Footsteps stomped down the stairs, and moments later, Nemain barged into the apartment, an amused expression on her face. Mikhail popped into existence in front of her, mist swirling off his shoulders, and the amusement in Nemain's emerald-green eyes evaporated instantly.

"I wasn't done with our conversation," he said.

"I don't care." She stepped around him. Magos let out a long-suffering sigh while Elisa covered her mouth to hide her grin. "Is there any food left?" Nemain asked as she eyed our plates.

"Oven," Elisa replied. "I turned it on warm. Figured you or the others from downstairs would come eventually."

Nemain grabbed a towel and pulled out a plate stacked high with pancakes and then reached in for the bacon. "Delicious," she purred.

"You haven't even eaten it yet," Mikhail pointed out.

Nemain ignored him as she grabbed another plate and stacked food on it. Finn watched them, wide-eyed, from where he still lay in the living room. He was just as confused by their behavior as I was.

"Elisa, can you rouse the rest of the vamp brats?" Nemain asked around mouthfuls of pancake and bacon.

"Yes . . . any particular reason?"

"We're going out."

Elisa perked up immediately. "Really? Where?"

"We're going to make a pit stop in one of the daemon realms to meet with Chamosh so he can apply the same sunlight spell he put on Magos on all of you." Nemain looked at me. "You up for meeting another valkyrie?"

I gaped at her and quickly closed my mouth so everyone didn't have to stare at my half-chewed food. Nemain could be speaking of only one valkyrie. "Sigrun?"

"Yup. She's been avoiding my calls the past two months, so I figured we'd take a more direct approach."

"Is that wise? Maybe she doesn't want to meet me."

"Sigrun is difficult, stubborn, and more than often deliberately obtuse——"

"Sounds like someone I know," Mikhail said, stealing a piece of bacon off Nemain's plate.

Nemain swiped at him, and he shied back. "It'll be good for her to meet you," Nemain said. "Even if she doesn't see it that way at first."

I chewed on my last piece of bacon, savoring the rich flavor. Nemain had mentioned Sigrun to me soon after I awakened my valkyrie magic, and I'd wanted to meet her ever since. Not only because I had questions only another valkyrie could answer, but because I wanted to become stronger. Finn and I were bonded for life. I would always be his guardian. The bond had been thrust on us because it was the only way to save my life at the time, but I didn't regret it. Finn's father was the most powerful fae in existence and he had an army of sidhe warriors. I needed to be stronger, and Sigrun could help me accomplish that.

"Okay." I collected the empty plates and took them over to the sink. "I'll get changed and then I'll be ready to go."

Elisa picked up the remaining pancakes and bacon. "I'll get the others up and ready. Meet downstairs in fifteen?"

Nemain nodded and raised her coffee as if it were a salute, while she shoved more food into her mouth with her other hand. The shifter really could eat. Mikhail tried to steal another piece of bacon, but Nemain was ready this time and slammed a dagger between his fingers, barely missing the skin.

"No weapons," Magos said in a measured tone.

Nemain curled her lip up at Mikhail and popped the last piece of bacon into her mouth. Mikhail rolled his eyes and picked up the last of the dishes, placing them in the sink.

Nemain swiveled around the stool and focused on Finn. "You up for an adventure today, kid?" He glanced up at her with his always too serious eyes and then looked at me, unsure how to answer.

"It'll be fun." I smiled confidently at him. "Isabeau and the others are coming along too."

Finn turned towards the silver grimalkin nestled in one of the chairs, a slightly larger black grimalkin curled around her. Luna stirred and blinked her lilac eyes sleepily. *We'll come too.*

"So basically everyone in the apartment then." Mikhail grunted and poured himself more coffee.

"You're not coming," Nemain said. "Eddie needs you and Magos for something."

Mikhail arched an eyebrow at her. "For what?"

"For something." Nemain arched an eyebrow back at him.

I stifled a laugh.

"Are you sure it's a good idea not taking backup with you?" Magos asked.

"I'm opening a gateway directly to Chamosh's workshop, and then we'll go straight to Sigrun's place. It'll be fine." Nemain shrugged. "We can't keep everyone locked up in this apartment forever, and this is safer than walking around town."

"Who is Chamosh?" I asked.

"He's the daemon that worked the spell that allows Magos to walk in the sun," Nemain explained. "It took some needling on my part, but I convinced him to do the same for Elisa and the other vamp kids. It shouldn't take too long." Nemain tossed a set of keys to Magos. "You can take my car."

"Meet you downstairs?" I asked. Nemain nodded and left along with the vampires. "I'm gonna get changed and then we'll go. Okay, Finn?"

His eyes flickered hesitantly towards the door. "Okay."

I opened the large armoire in my bedroom and looked at my options. What exactly did a newbie valkyrie wear when going to meet an older valkyrie in hopes of convincing them to be her mentor? I tugged on the plain black T-shirt I was wearing. Nothing in the closet was that impressive. I didn't have any armor or fancy clothes. Nemain's friend Kaysea had acquired most of the clothes for me, and they consisted of comfy stuff to wear around the house. Finding clothing that worked with my wings was challenging, and Kaysea had had some things tailored for me and was working on more. Deciding the shirt was good enough, I swapped out the sweatpants for fitted but stretchy dark grey pants that had plenty of deep pockets.

My hand hovered over a matching dark grey cloak. Even growing up in the mountains, the cold had rarely bothered me, and now that I had awoken my valkyrie nature, it bothered me even less. If anything, I always felt a little warm. I closed the armoire, leaving the cloak behind. My wings would be enough to keep me warm. Snatching up a pair of black combat boots, I headed back out to the living room.

Finn was waiting, Jinx and Luna at his side. The silver grimalkin had helped raise Finn, and she was protective of him. I gave her a warm smile as I reached down to tug on my boots.

Nervous? Luna asked.

"A little," I answered out loud. My telepathic skills weren't that strong despite Nemain being pretty sure most valkyries were good at communicating telepathically. One of the many things on the list to ask Sigrun. I glanced at Jinx. His golden eyes appeared bored and slightly annoyed. I'd learned quickly upon moving in that Jinx valued his nap time a great deal. But he valued Luna more. Luna wanted to go on this trip; therefore, Jinx rousted himself from his nap to tag along. "You've met Sigrun, right?"

Yes.

"Do you think she'll agree to help me?"

I don't know. But if anyone can berate her into doing so, it's Nemain.

9

Jinx trotted towards the apartment door and used his magic to swing it open.

Luna brushed against Finn's legs and followed Jinx down the stairs. I held out my hand to Finn, and he gripped it tightly as we followed the grimalkins.

Chapter Two

THE APARTMENT DOOR was open when we reached the bottom landing, and I closed it behind us. Misha greeted me from the kitchen. Like Elisa, Misha had straight black hair, pale skin, and dark indigo blue eyes. I'd assumed they were siblings when we first met, but they told me they weren't sure. Elisa, Misha, and Damon had grown up together from a young age, with Isabeau joining their group later on. The Vampire Council had kept them contained their entire lives, and they had no idea who their parents were. But because of their upbringing, they considered each other siblings. With Elisa and Misha, that might be true on a literal level.

"Ready for a day of fun?" Misha grinned at me.

I flinched as Isabeau's high-pitched squeal rang across the living room. "I'm curious what the daemon realm is like." I rubbed at my ear, trying to get the ringing to stop. "Have you been there before?"

"Yeah," Misha said, grabbing a piece of bacon and wrapping a pancake around it. "Only a couple times, though. Vampires aren't exactly well liked by daemons, or anyone for that matter, so Nemain is careful about where she takes us."

The source of the high-pitched squealing skipped into the kitchen, her brown curls bouncing with the movement, and she slid to a stop in front of Misha. He smiled at the young vampire girl and handed over the pancake-wrapped bacon.

"Thank you!" Isabeau chirped and spun towards the living room. "Finn, you have to try this!"

I watched with a bemused smile as Isabeau tore the pancake roll in half and gave Finn a piece. He tentatively took a small bite, eyes lighting up as he chewed.

"It's good, right?" Isabeau said, inhaling her piece in two bites. "Elisa makes the best breakfast. Damon and Misha can't cook anything, but they're good for ordering pizza."

"I'm so glad we're good for something," Misha said dryly.

"It's good to have a purpose in life." I nodded solemnly.

"She jokes!" Damon announced as he lumbered into the kitchen. Grey eyes with a hint of blue met mine, and he grinned. "I was worried when you first arrived that you'd be too serious to fit in with us, but it appears there's hope for you yet!"

Elisa breezed into the kitchen and smacked him upside the head. "Give her a break. She's been through a lot and is still adjusting to everything." She reached into one of the cupboards and pulled out a box of crackers. Misha handed her a small plastic box, and she poured some crackers into it. "Snacks for the kids in case they get hungry," she explained when she saw my questioning look.

"Oooh!" Damon reached for the crackers, but Elisa swatted his hand away.

"They're for the kids," she scolded. "You're seventeen years old. You don't get snacks."

"I still want snacks, though." Damon gave her a hurt expression. I had to admit, he was really good at it. With his warm brown skin and light brown hair, always in a casual state of disarray around his face, it was hard to not smile back at

Damon or give in to his pouting expressions. He was friendly and inviting, and I'd liked him right off the bat. I liked all of them. I just didn't always know how to act around them.

The vampire kids had their dynamic figured out already. Elisa was in charge as the oldest, Damon and Misha followed her lead, and all of them took care of Isabeau. Finn and I had spent most of our time on the run and fighting for our lives. I didn't know how to act in a kitchen where we were arguing over who got snacks.

Elisa noticed the change in my demeanor and tossed the box at Damon. "If you want to bring some, you'll have to pack them yourself." She walked over and stood by me. "I packed enough for Finn, too."

"Umm, thanks," I said awkwardly. "Nemain should be here soon. Mikhail and Magos aren't coming because Eddie needs them for something."

The door opened, saving me from trying to think of something else to say, and Nemain breezed in. Her twin swords were on her back, and I spotted at least six daggers strapped to her in various places as well. Apparently, despite her words about this trip being no big deal, she still felt inclined to dress like she was going into battle.

"Y'all ready?"

"Yes," Elisa answered, stuffing the bag of crackers and a couple of bottles of water into her backpack. Finn bent down to pick up Luna and came over to me. Jinx leapt up to Nemain's shoulder.

"Watch the claws!" she snapped. "Just drop your glamour and go in your fae form. I'm not carrying you the whole time."

The floor of his workshop has a weird texture. I don't like it.

"It's just dust leftover from grinding the stone and gems he uses. It's barely noticeable."

It feels like sand. You know how I feel about sand.

Nemain sighed and opened a gateway, revealing a large

building made of steel grey stones. Sunlight poured onto the street between us and the dark wooden door leading inside. Out of the corner of my eye, I could see the vamp kids shift uncomfortably. All the apartments had floor-to-ceiling windows covered by blackout curtains all day to keep them sheltered. Direct contact with sunlight would burn their skin. It wouldn't kill them right away, but Elisa told me it felt like holding your arm over a fire. They also couldn't see well in the brightness of daylight.

"Sorry, Chamosh would have a conniption if I opened a gateway in the middle of his workshop," Nemain apologized. "I'll open the door so you can run in. It's only a few steps."

"It'll be fine," Elisa said. "We've all been exposed to sunlight for far longer than this." Something dark in her tone gave me pause. I knew about Elisa and the others' history, but only the general details. What exactly had the Vampire Council done to them? Elisa grabbed a throw blanket off the couch and tugged it over Isabeau's head. "Just like we practiced before, remember?"

Isabeau nodded under the blanket. "I remember."

Nemain walked onto the bright street and raised the iron knocker on the door, letting it fall once. Heavy footsteps sounded, and the door swung open, revealing a large stocky daemon with dark red skin, solid black eyes, and curling horns. He reminded me of Zareen, a bartender at Pele's pub and a friend of Nemain's. I didn't know Zareen all that well. She had stopped by a couple times, usually in the company of Kaysea, but she was sweet and seemed to be perpetually cheerful.

This daemon was not.

His obsidian black eyes glared at Nemain beneath dark bushy eyebrows, and he raised them and glared at all of us, still waiting on the other side of the gateway. His lips tugged downward, and he grunted and swore under his breath, stomping back inside.

Nemain looked over her shoulder at us. "That was Chamosh's way of saying hello." She took a step to the side and gestured towards the open door. "Come on in. Don't break anything because I can't afford it."

I stepped through the gateway first and Finn followed me, still holding Luna. Instead of going inside, I stopped halfway between the gateway and the building. It was only about ten feet. With the afternoon sun at my back, I stretched my wings high and wide. It didn't create shade exactly, but it helped a little.

Finn tilted his head back so he could study my wings and how they shone even brighter with the sunlight bouncing off the golden feathers. "Pretty," he said softly, his yellow and green eyes shining.

Elisa stood in front of the gateway, still sheltered from the sun on the apartment side. She was staring at me wide-eyed; awe and something else flickered on her face as she took in my glittering gold wings. Her gaze snagged on mine, and we stared at each other. I was pretty sure I had stopped breathing.

"Quit checking out the valkyrie," Misha called out and shoved Elisa forward. "You can dwell on your little fantasy once we're inside."

What?

Elisa whirled around, ignoring the steam already rising off her skin, and grabbed Misha by the shirt. She yanked him forward and flung him twenty feet *away* from the door. He crashed down and flipped over a couple of times before sitting upright and shaking his head. He glared at Elisa and snapped out of existence, appearing a second later inside the building.

I blinked. I'd known about Misha's ability, but I hadn't realized Elisa was that strong. And what fantasy was he talking about?

Elisa walked past me, very carefully not looking at me as she joined Misha where he stood a few feet in the hallway behind the door. She punched his shoulder, and he stumbled back a few steps, rubbing it as he grumbled something at her.

"Again," Nemain said patiently. "I can't afford to pay for anything you break. So unless you want to be on loan to a daemon for a few weeks to work off the debt, I suggest you behave."

Damon guided Isabeau into the building; like Elisa, he ignored the steam rising off his skin as he calmly but quickly entered the building. My nose twitched at the faint smell of burning skin, but the minor blisters on the vampires' skin were already healing. Nemain closed the gateway as Finn and I followed the others down the hallway.

Nemain ushered us further into the building, which opened into a large workshop. Like the outside, the inside was all exposed dark grey stone. Despite the lack of windows, it was brightly lit by glowing spheres that floated around the ceiling. Nemain strode confidently into the workshop and started talking to Chamosh, who was ignoring all of us while he picked through gems from a large bin that rested on one of the many workbenches scattered around the floor. We all stood there, gawking at the space in front of us.

Somehow it managed to be both highly organized and chaotic at the same time. From the little I knew of daemons, that seemed to fit with their general personality traits. Half a dozen workbenches were haphazardly set up in the center of the space, some with tools on them, others with bins of gems and stones. The back half of the building had a large forge with a blazing fire. I didn't see any weapons scattered around, so I wasn't exactly sure what he was using it for. On either side of us were shelves containing more gems, stones, crystals, and other materials I didn't recognize.

Isabeau started bouncing towards some shelves, but Elisa grabbed her and held her back.

"Don't touch anything," the daemon barked. After giving

Nemain one last dirty look, he dropped the large scarlet gem he'd been studying and walked over to us. "It's bad enough you came here and asked me to work that spell before," he growled. "But now you're asking me to do it again for a paltry sum! I'm not running a vampire charity house here."

"Don't be rude," Nemain said in a bored tone. "Everyone, this is Chamosh. He is the one responsible for Magos being able to walk in the sun, and he's been ever so kind to extend that working to all of you." The large and imposing daemon scowled at the sarcasm-laden words. But before he could respond, Elisa stepped forward.

"We thank you for taking time out of your schedule to help us with this. I know someone of your skill is highly sought after and that this magic is far simpler than what you would typically work on." Elisa gave him an earnest smile and placed a hand on her chest. I fought to keep my face neutral at Elisa's performance. "It means the world to us, and we will be forever grateful to you."

I didn't miss that she had chosen her words carefully so she didn't owe the daemon anything specifically. Gratitude could simply mean being polite. The daemons weren't as bad as the fae who were more than happy to take advantage of a poorly phrased statement, but I suspected the daemons weren't that different either. Elisa had been spending time with Pele, and it seemed she was quickly picking up Pele's gift of words.

Chamosh eyed her, his gruff expression thawing slightly. "What is your name, child?"

"Elisa."

The daemon grunted and moved to a different workshop bench where several tools were laid out. "I just finished up a project anyway and had some time this afternoon." He raised a long thin piece of iron with what looked like a symbol of the sun on one end. "I still have most of the supplies from last time. I just need to power it up again."

"Wonderful," Elisa said. "We'll stay out of your way, and I'll keep everyone out of trouble while you work. Simply let us know what you need from us when it is time."

Chamosh grunted again. I was beginning to suspect that was his primary form of communication. He moved towards the furnace, shoving the end of the iron over some burning coals. Alarm shot through me, and my eyes darted to Isabeau. Were they planning on branding the little girl with the spell? I knew nothing about daemon magic or how it worked other than they were on par with fae magic in most ways, but this felt barbaric. Nobody else in the room seemed concerned about this turn of events, though.

It doesn't hurt. Luna's kind voice filled my head. *Daemons work magic differently than the fae. They mostly rely on fire and earth magic to craft their spells. He'll cast the spell on the iron brand while it burns, but he'll cut off the flames and heat before pressing it to their skin. It will leave behind a slightly upraised tattoo.*

I relaxed a little and gave her a grateful nod.

"Let's take a walk," Nemain announced, turning to face me. "Elisa and Jinx can watch over the others. I'd like some fresh air, and this will give you and Finn a chance to see more of the daemon realm."

Why do I have to stay here? Jinx complained.

Because Finn isn't going to leave Luna behind, and I want one of you to stay here, Nemain replied. I really needed to practice communicating telepathically. Nemain wasn't a strong telepath, and she had to work a little harder to push the thoughts to include me. I seemed to be making her life more difficult at every turn without meaning to.

Jinx looked at where Luna was still curled up in Finn's arms. *Fine*, he grumbled. *But don't be gone long.*

We'll be back in twenty minutes, Nemain promised. *We're just going to walk around a couple of blocks and come back.*

Jinx leapt from where he'd been sitting on Nemain's

shoulder to a nearby shelf, weaving between a few boxes and perching midway down. His golden eyes glowed against his black fur.

Nemain waved Finn and me forward, and we followed her back down the hallway to the front door. Out on the street, Nemain tilted her head back and stood there for a moment, breathing in the warm afternoon air before tilting her head towards us. "I hate the way daemon workshops smell. The sulfur they use in their spells makes my nose itch."

"I noticed that. Is it worse for you because you're a shifter?"

"Yes." Nemain shrugged. "It'd be even worse if I was in my feline form. It probably bothers the vampires as well, but their sense of smell isn't nearly as sensitive as mine. They rely more on sight and hearing."

A few daemons ambled down the street, curiosity brimming on their faces as they passed. Finn bent down and set Luna on her feet where she promptly dropped her glamour. Where a ten-pound cat had stood before was now a hundred-pound feline with a sleek muscular body and long claws that jutted out as she flexed her paws. If we didn't draw attention before, we certainly would now.

I glanced around the street to see how the daemons would react to a shifter, a valkyrie, and two fae beings in their midst, but aside from a few glancing looks, none of them seemed to mind. I turned my attention to the street.

"This wasn't what I expected," I said as I took in the buildings and random decor.

Nemain snickered and walked down the wide street at a leisurely pace. "The fae build their towns and cities with nature in mind, using the natural landscape as the blueprint for how the buildings will be laid out," she explained. "Did you ever go to any of the cities in Tír na mBeo?"

"Yes, only a few times. Cathair na Sneachta wasn't that

large, but it was definitely far grander than any of the mountain villages. The city streets wound around large trees and most of the buildings' sides were covered with vines. It was beautiful." My eyes skimmed the buildings that lined the streets. Not a plant in sight. "This feels . . . lifeless."

"After spending your entire life in the fae realm, I understand why you would feel that way."

We approached a four-way intersection with a large fountain at its center. A stone tree rose out of the water, its branches extending just beyond the rim of the fountain. Incredibly detailed leaves adorned its branches made of some type of copper mineral that glittered in the sun. It wasn't alive. Every part of it was made of stone and minerals, but it was captivating all the same. I didn't realize I'd moved towards it until my knees bumped into the fountain.

Finn moved to stand by me, and Luna leapt up onto the rim and peered down into the water. "Feel it," Nemain said from where she stood behind us.

I reached up and felt the tip of a branch. It was warm from the sun, but I could feel the buzz of magic. Finn bumped against me, and I lifted him up to perch on my shoulder. Tentatively, he reached out and lightly touched the pointed tip of a leaf. Unlike Finn, I couldn't see magic, only feel it. I wished I knew what the tree looked like to him. As it was, it appeared magnificent to me, but given the magic pulsing from it, it was likely even more spectacular to him.

"It's alive," Finn said in wonder.

"Most beings think of the fae as being more in touch with nature and magic and the daemons as being the practical species," Nemain said, coming to stand beside us. "But the daemons are crafty. They never tried to directly compete with the fae; instead, they carved a path that set them apart. Equal in power but not in direct competition. If you want a beautiful silver dagger that will poison anyone stabbed with it while it glistens beautifully in the sunlight, then you go to the fae. But if you want a well-crafted, borderline plain-looking dagger that will leap back into your hand after it's thrown, then you go to the daemons."

Nemain ran her fingers along a stony branch. "But the daemons are every bit as capable of creating beautiful, complex things as the fae are. I first saw this tree three centuries ago, and it was barely my height, and now..." She raised her hands and gestured towards the branches that towered above us, stretching towards the sun. "The daemons came very close to extinction once, and they fought hard for every inch of their lives. Their cities might seem lifeless at first glance, but you'll learn just how untrue that is the more time you spend in them."

We continued walking around the block, Nemain pointing out buildings and other things she thought would interest us. The more we explored, the more I saw how wrong my original assessment of the daemon city as cold and lifeless was. Even without being able to see the magic that ran deeply throughout the city, the complex architecture entranced me. Daemons clearly loved geometric designs. No two buildings were alike, and different types of stone and minerals created patterns on many of the exteriors. Above us, tunnels made of stone and glass stretched between the taller buildings, creating even more pathways.

Daemons passed us, some giving wary or curious glances, but nothing more. Until one daemon with ice-blue eyes slowed down as they approached us. They had a cold androgynous beauty to them, and I started to move between them and Finn, but Nemain caught my eye and shook her head. The daemon knelt in front of Finn, the beads in their long black braids clicking against each other. Finn stood perfectly still as the daemon held out their hands, clasped together as if holding something between them. Slowly, they opened it, revealing a hawk made of small intricate gears and strips of metal.

Finn cocked his head to the side as he pondered the metal bird, and magic pulsed from the daemon. The hawk opened its beak and let out a small shriek and flapped its wings, flying from the daemon's palm to Finn's shoulder. The hawk butted its head against his cheek and let out another squawk. Finn's eyes grew almost comically wide as he met the eyes of the daemon. The daemon grinned and brushed off their hands, rising and continuing down the street without a word.

I looked at Nemain while Finn coaxed the small hawk onto his finger.

She shrugged. "Children are cherished in daemon society, even children of other species. The fae are similar but more reserved about it; many of them put higher expectations on their own children. The daemons love their children unconditionally."

An unexpected jolt of anger hit me, and I clenched my hands into fists. Beck's parents hadn't loved him unconditionally. The fae boy had grown up with me and most of my childhood memories involved him. His parents had been disappointed in his small amount of magic and that had led him to betraying me and Finn. My nails bit into my skin. I'd killed him for what he'd done but that did nothing to alleviate the anger. I thought he'd been my friend.

"The fae have conditions," I said bitterly.

"Not all," Nemain hedged. "But it's true for many, especially those of the Tuatha Dé Danann."

The memory of Beck's head toppling from his shoulders flashed in my mind. I'd done that. Killed my friend with no hesitation after the breadth of his betrayal was made clear. I'd been waiting for the guilt to come, but it never did. Only the anger remained. Nemain walked beside me, and I studied her out of the corner of my eye. Her face was pensive but troubled. It had been her sword I'd used to kill Beck. She'd tossed it to me, knowing full well what I was going to do. None of them had judged me for what I'd done. Except the wolf.

"Do you miss him?" I asked, the words slipping out. I inwardly flinched. We'd all been very careful not to talk about Andrei, and here I was, bringing him up out of nowhere.

"Who?"

I paused, desperately trying to think of another name to throw out that would make sense but not coming up with anything.

Nemain, seeing my hesitation, took a guess. "Andrei?" At my nod, she pursed her lips, her bright green eyes dimming. "I do. Most of my friends think I'm a fool for it. They thought I was an idiot for becoming involved with him in the first place." A wry smile played across her lips, but her eyes remained hollow. "You and Finn came into my life at an odd time. I've spent most of my life hiding my magic, trying not to be noticed by anyone with too much power, particularly the fae and daemons. Andrei made me happy. I knew he would never use me for my magic or political gain. He was kind and funny. Being with him kept the darkness at bay."

"You loved him?"

"I did. I still do."

My brows bunched together. "Then why did you end it?"

"Because when Andrei and I first got together, I thought I could keep him out of my world." Nemain glanced at me. "Our world. You know the path we're all on now. I'm essentially the caretaker of four Apex vampire children, all of whom are still wanted by the Vampire Council. And I'm part of a prophecy involving the son of the exiled fae king, who is also my ward of sorts now. That alone would have caused tension between me and Andrei and put him in danger. Then there was the small matter of me killing his sister's lover."

I winced.

"The nail in the coffin was when I knew I'd likely have to join the Unseelie Court. Andrei would have stayed. He loved me as much as I loved him. But that love would have turned to hate over the years as he watched me do whatever I needed to keep Finn safe."

The pain in her voice was my fault. Finn was my responsibility, but I'd failed in keeping him safe so Nemain had been forced to step up. How different could her life have been if Finn and I had never entered it? Or if I'd been more skilled at protecting him? Maybe she and the wolf could have gotten a happy ending.

"I'm sorry." The words felt so inadequate, but I didn't know what else to say.

Nemain halted and spun to face me. Her vertical pupils were barely visible in the bright afternoon sun, and her emerald eyes blazed once more. "Listen to me carefully, Bryn. What happened was not your fault. I was already on the radar of the Warlock Circle long before the two of you strolled into my life. Furthermore, I am the daughter of The Morrigan and The Erlking. That truth would have come out eventually because the Unseelie Queen has had her eyes on me for a long time. She was merely biding her time. You are young and will hopefully have a long life. It is impossible to avoid bad or impossible choices in life. Things will happen that you will feel guilty for, and you will be right to feel that way. This is *not* one of them. Do you understand?"

She waited until I jerked my head in a nod. "Good. Let's go back. The others should be ready. We have a valkyrie to track down."

Chapter Three

THE REALM NEMAIN took us to after leaving Chamosh's workshop was a stark contrast to the daemon streets we'd just walked through. She opened a gateway into a meadow filled with white and blue blossoms. A lone cottage sat among the flowers, with a slightly larger building behind it. The tops of trees rose behind the buildings revealing the start of a forest. I could just barely make out the outline of vast mountains off in the distance. But there were no signs of any other buildings or people living here.

Apparently, Sigrun liked her privacy.

Jinx and Nemain were arguing about something while Finn pondered the large sprawling tree that stood in front of the cottage where all the vampires were gathered. We had come directly from the workshop, and they had yet to step fully into the sunlight. Seeing that Luna was with Finn, I walked over to join Elisa and the others. They were all standing in the shade with strained expressions, as if they still couldn't accept that the sun would no longer harm them. Slowly, they held their hands up, letting the sunbeams filtering through the leaves play across their skin. When Isabeau decided to skip away from the safety of the tree, Elisa moved to grab her, only to hold herself back.

"It's okay," I told her quietly after moving to stand by her side.

"I didn't think it would hit us like this," Elisa said. "Obviously, I knew what the spell would do, and I've seen Mikhail and Magos walk in the sunlight. But I've spent the last two decades of my life fearing it."

"Have you spent much time in sunlight before the spell?" I asked carefully.

Elisa fell silent. It was Misha who answered. "The magic of Apex vampires isn't always passed on to their offspring. The Council has been working hard the last century to create more of us, and they didn't want to waste any time on vampire children who didn't inherit the traits of their genetic donors."

My expression hardened. Not parents, none of them had parents. Only vampires who had donated their genetics so the Council could raise powerful soldiers subservient to them.

"It can take years for our magic to manifest, but the Council is impatient. They allow us five years after we're born, then they start testing us." Misha curled his fingers into a fist and held it out fully in the sun. "Exposing us to sunlight is their favorite tactic. The pain was beyond anything I can describe. They'd leave you in a room by yourself for hours with only your screams for company. It would only get worse as your magic began to run out from healing the burns, and then the hunger would kick in. It felt like dying."

"All of you went through that?" I asked.

All three vampires watched Isabeau prancing in a circle around Finn, trying to convince him to climb the tree with her. "Not all of us," Damon said.

So, this was why they had escaped when they did. Isabeau would be turning seven soon. They had escaped to spare her what they had all survived. Now, with Chamosh's spell in place,

Isabeau would never know what it was like to be tortured by sunlight. I felt a kinship settle into place between me and the three vampires. They had chosen to protect Isabeau at all costs, the same way I had chosen to protect Finn.

"I'll help you keep her safe," I told them quietly.

"And we will help you keep Finn safe," Elisa promised, both Misha and Damon nodding in agreement.

"Then just stay here," Nemain snapped at Jinx, throwing up her hands as she talked to the house. "Come on, kids!"

"Do you think she'll ever stop referring to us as kids?" I asked Elisa.

"I've asked her that same question." Elisa smiled at me, and my heart flipped. "She said she had four centuries on us, and we would always be kids to her."

I frowned. "Wasn't Andrei only in his thirties?"

Misha snorted. "You should point that out to her."

"Just give us a warning first so we can make popcorn," Damon added.

"I think I'll keep that observation to myself." I cracked a grin.

Finn came running over to me and grabbed my hand, pulling me towards the cottage. I wiped my other hand against my pants. What if Sigrun was angry about us coming here and refused to help me? Nemain didn't think it would be a good idea to go to the other valkyries, but I didn't fully understand why. If Sigrun refused to help me, I wouldn't have a choice. I had no idea how to use my magic, and I needed someone to teach me.

Nemain banged on the solid wood door. "Open the damn door, Sigrun!"

I flinched. This didn't seem like a good way for me to meet the valkyrie for the first time. Elisa patted my shoulder in sympathy, as if she could read my thoughts. Magic flowed out of Finn and the front door swung open.

Nemain pulled her fist back and gave Finn a small mischievous grin. "You're really handy, kid."

Drawing in a deep breath, I followed Nemain inside, Finn still holding my hand. I didn't know if he was doing it because he needed the support or if he thought I did. Either way, I made no move to let go. We all crowded into a small but homey living room. Two well-worn chairs were set in front of the currently unlit fireplace, but I could still smell the traces of smoke in the room, as if it had settled into all the blankets and furniture. Weapons lined the wall, along with a few shelves for books and other knickknacks. Not a sound came from anywhere in the house.

"She must be out on a job," Nemain muttered. "We'll wait a few hours and see if she comes back; otherwise, we'll return tomorrow."

Jinx stalked over to one of the chairs near the fireplace. As his weight shifted to his hindquarters in preparation to jump, a brown, medium-sized cat appeared out of nowhere in the chair.

"Fuck!" Damon jumped back from where he'd been standing close to the chair.

"Language!" Elisa hissed.

Jinx's ears were pinned back, and a long hiss poured out of him. *I thought there was a noxious odor in here.*

You're just smelling your over-inflated ego. It stinks up any room you're in, a deep voice grumbled.

"Hello, Viggo," Nemain said with a sigh. "We're here for Sigrun."

Obviously. The brown cat rose to a sitting position. It was hard to tell with his long, fluffy coat, but he looked a little smaller than Jinx in his fae form. I pegged him at around eighty pounds. His light green eyes roamed over each of us, but when he spotted my golden wings wrapped around me like a cloak, his eyes widened. He whirled in the chair and glared at Nemain. *Leave.*

Hurt slammed into me, but I kept it off my face.

"I don't take orders from you, skogkatt," Nemain said. "Where is Sigrun?"

We don't want anything to do with valkyrie business. You know this.

"This isn't valkyrie business, it's my business," Nemain argued. "I will explain to Sigrun. Tell me where she is."

The cat's tufted ears swiveled back and forth. A faint tremble ran through his limbs as he leaned against the back of the chair. He was trying to hide it, but something was wrong.

"Are you hurt?" I asked softly.

Those green eyes focused on me and then on Finn, who was still gripping my hand. Horror flickered through them. *What have you done? You bonded with a fae? And one who is tainted? I can see the devourer magic swirling around him. He's an abomination and shouldn't exist!*

I stepped towards the chair, hands balled in tight fists, as twin growls ripped out of Luna and Jinx. Before anyone could rip the skogkatt from his chair, a strange feeling filtered through the room. My mind felt light, like I'd stood up too fast. I was vaguely aware of both grimalkins hunkering down to the ground, their fur standing on end. Misha and Damon were clutching their heads in their hands. My attention immediately went to Finn to make sure he was okay, assuming the magic was coming from him, but he wasn't looking at the skogkatt. I followed his gaze and went still.

Isabeau was staring at Viggo. Her hazel eyes has turned solid black with jagged white lines streaked through them like fractured marble. I didn't know what she was doing to the skogkatt, but he seemed to be locked into place where he still stood on the chair, face frozen in terror.

Finn released my hand and walked over to the young vampire girl. He touched her shoulder, and she slowly turned her head and met his gaze. Whatever communication passed between them was kept from the rest of us. She blinked once and her eyes gradually faded back to their usual brown with flecks of green. Viggo sagged on the chair, released from whatever magic she had just used on him.

"Do not be mean to my friend," Isabeau said, sounding a lot older than six years. Without another word, she turned and headed back outside.

Elisa cut a glance at Misha and Damon, and they followed her out. Finn looked at me, and I nodded. He joined them outside. Viggo started to rise to his feet but was knocked back down as a wave of magic lashed out of Luna. She eyed the skogkatt coldly and went outside.

"You will find we're all monsters here," Nemain said lightly. "And we protect our own."

I may have overreacted, Viggo said stiffly.

Not exactly an apology. Part of me still wanted to tear the skogkatt apart, limb from limb, for calling Finn an abomination. But I needed Sigrun's help, so I slowly pulled the rage deep inside, letting it settle in my core.

"The story about how Bryn"—Nemain waved a hand at me—"and Finn came into our lives is a long one, and I'm not telling it twice. Where is Sigrun?"

Some devourers have encroached on our territory. We took out most of them yesterday, but one of them managed to surprise me and took a chunk of my magic before the dog could get it off me.

"So Gunnar saved your ass yet again?" Nemain snickered.

I would have had it! Viggo snarled. *We've noticed some other odd things in the forests west of here. Sigrun took the dog out this morning to make sure the devourers were all taken care of and that nothing else was poking around. She commanded me to stay so I could heal. They haven't returned yet.*

He hid it well, but I could tell he was worried. It didn't make me any less pissed off at him.

"Where did you find the devourers yesterday?"

Two miles to the northwest.

My eyebrows shot up. "That close?"

Yes.

"Let's go see if we can find them," Nemain said. "It'll be good for the vamp brats to stretch their legs."

"Is that safe?" I asked, not loving the idea of taking Finn and Isabeau into a possible fight with devourers.

Nemain shrugged. "If things get hairy, I'll open a gateway back to the apartment. But I've seen the devourers that roam this realm. They're not that bad. Jinx can take them down single-handedly." Viggo stiffened at the insult, and Nemain laughed. "Rest up, Viggo. Wouldn't want your delicate self to get injured again."

The skogkatt let out an annoyed growl as we joined the others outside.

"What do you think?" I asked Elisa. She'd remained quiet during the entire exchange. I had no doubt she was thinking about Isabeau's display of magic and trying to figure out what it meant.

"I'm beginning to think all feline species are assholes." She cut a quick glance at Nemain. "Except feline shifters, of course."

"No, we're definitely assholes too," Nemain said.

"But you and Finn should be prepared for that type of response from others," Elisa said. "I know it's difficult to hear, and it makes you want to rip the person to shreds. But doing so will rarely make the situation better and will prove the fears of those people to be correct. Which in the long run will only hurt Finn more."

"So you think I should just tolerate people calling Finn an abomination to his face?"

Elisa's calculating blue eyes fell on me. "I'm saying you should smile in response and tell them that perhaps they should choose their words more wisely. You're a valkyrie, Bryn. All you have to do is flex those golden wings to draw attention to your strong build and deep well of magic. Everything about you radiates power, and you haven't even fully come into your magic yet. Imagine what you'll be like a year from now when you're fully trained. You'll be more stunning than you already are."

Stunning. The beautiful vampire thought *I* was stunning. Every part of me focused on fighting the blush that wanted to bloom across my cheeks.

"If anyone is foolish enough to continue insulting Finn after that," Elisa continued, "carve their heart from their chest and burn the body so no one will ever find it. Or better yet, let me or one of the guys know so we can have some dinner. Blood shouldn't be wasted, especially if it's powerful blood."

"Your pragmatism makes me so proud," Nemain said.

"Thank you," I told Elisa. "I'll have to work on flexing my wings in impressive manners."

"You can practice on me anytime."

I stumbled, and only Nemain shooting out a steadying hand kept me from falling flat on my face. Gods, what was wrong with me? Elisa just grinned at me and trotted ahead to where Damon and Misha were trying in vain to get Isabeau and Finn out of the tree.

"Smooth move, valkyrie," Nemain teased. "Your face is still bright red by the way."

"You're not helping!" I snapped and stomped off towards the tree, Nemain's laughter following in my wake.

Chapter Four

"WHAT ARE THEY?" I asked, as we studied the aftermath of yesterday's fight. Small furry bodies were scattered around the tall grass. Their matted fur was a creamy tan with light green stripes that allowed them to blend into the dry grass exceptionally well. I knelt down next to one for a closer look. Its long arms ended with three curved talons, and a blunt muzzle protruded from its furry head. On its own, it probably wouldn't be much of a threat, even with its devourer magic. But there had to be at least thirty of them scattered around us.

"Sigrun just calls them meindyr," Nemain said. "This realm is full of them, but they're fairly harmless. There are some other nastier devourer species here, but she's hunted most of them down. The few that remain are far from here."

"Why does she live here?" I asked, brushing my hands against my pants as I stood. "Aren't there other realms she could live in that wouldn't require her to constantly be battling against devourers?"

"I'm gonna let her explain that one." Nemain looked at Elisa, who was trying to keep Isabeau from poking at one of the bodies. "Up for testing out your wolf skills? Sigrun and Gunnar likely would have gone on foot from here."

"Sure." One moment, Elisa was standing there and in the next a large black wolf had taken her place. She shook her fur once and trotted around us, nose to the ground while she shuffled through all the scents. Nemain watched her work with a pained expression before following after Elisa when she veered to the northeast.

"She's sad," Finn said next to me. I hadn't even heard him move. Kid could be eerily quiet sometimes.

"She misses Andrei," Isabeau said from my other side, causing me to jump.

"I wish you both would stop doing that," I growled.

Isabeau laughed and ran after Nemain. "Come on, Finn! I'll race you to the hill!" Finn looked after the vampire girl, clearly unsure about what to do.

"Come on, kid," Damon said. "We'll distract Isabeau to give you an advantage. Then you can lord it over her for the next week that she was too slow to make it to the top first."

Misha grinned and teleported directly in front of Isabeau. "Boo!" She shrieked and slammed on the brakes. Misha teleported again, this time behind her, and tugged on one of her curls. Isabeau whirled and tried to tackle him, only for the dark-haired vampire to disappear again. Finn took a few steps forward and broke out into a run, passing a still shrieking Isabeau, who only screamed louder when the fae boy took the lead.

Damon jogged after them, leaving me alone with the grimalkins. "Do you think Nemain is okay?" I asked Jinx. He'd known her longer than anyone, and he wouldn't sugarcoat things. The grumpy grimalkin didn't know the meaning of the word.

Nemain survives. She always does, Jinx said. *It will take some time for her to adjust to the new way of things. Neither of us really knows what it means to belong to a fae court. She made the right decision to send the wolf away. If he stayed, someone would have eventually targeted him as a way to get to her. And that . . . that I'm not sure Nemain would have survived. Not after Myrna.*

I wanted to ask who Myrna was, but Jinx trotted off after the others, leaving Luna and me to follow. I made a mental note to ask Elisa about it later. Joining the others at the top of the hill, I studied what lay before us. The meadow ended at the bottom of the hill, a vast forest of conifer trees stretching as far as the eye could see. It reminded me a little of the forests I'd grown up in, but these trees were smaller and not as densely packed.

Elisa shifted back to her vampire form, her clothing still perfect and not a hair out of place. I still didn't understand how that worked exactly. "Assuming the trail continues going in the direction it has been, it leads straight into those woods."

Nemain glanced up at the late afternoon sun approaching the horizon. "We still have a couple hours of daylight left. We'll go a little further and if we don't see anything, we'll head back."

"And leave Sigrun out there alone?" I asked.

"Nothing has managed to kill Sigrun yet," Nemain said dryly. "I doubt a few devourers are up to the task."

Somehow I didn't find that all that comforting.

"I heard something," Misha said. Elisa, once again in her wolf form, stopped in her tracks. Her ears perking forward and swiveling to the side, listening for whatever Misha had heard.

Nemain moved in front of them. "Everyone stay behind me," she commanded and set off again.

We followed her silently as we wound our way through the woods. The trees in this forest had shallow roots, which caused uneven footing. If we had to run, it wouldn't go so well for us. Even walking, we had to choose our footing carefully. Jinx and Luna had it easier. They had leapt into the trees the second we'd entered the forest and traveled along the branches. After a quarter mile, we approached a clearing and Nemain stopped.

Elisa, however, was so absorbed in following the scent trail that she kept going. My instincts screamed at me, and I ran towards Elisa as an unseen force slammed into her, knocking her off her feet. Elisa snarled as she tumbled with whatever had attacked her. The scent of her blood filled the clearing, and my vision turned red.

"Gunnar! Stop!" Nemain screamed. She ran towards Elisa and her invisible attacker but didn't pull out any weapons. My magic started to rise, and so did my panic. I didn't know how to control it. Last time I'd let it loose, dozens of fae devourers had been in front of me and I'd had a clear target. Even then, Jinx and Finn had held up a shield over everyone to protect them. Elisa let out a yelp of pain, and my magic surged once more even as I tried to pull it back while running towards her.

A sharp whistle sounded through the clearing, and everyone stopped. A tall, broad-shouldered woman entered the clearing from the right. Even with the fading sunlight, her golden wings stood out against her midnight black skin. She strode through the clearing at a leisurely pace and I couldn't help but be awed by her. I thought I would be prepared to see another valkyrie but seeing the strength she emitted hit me harder than I thought. This was what I wanted to be.

Tearing my gaze away from the valkyrie, I darted to Elisa's side. The black wolf slowly rose to her feet, a deep growl rumbling from her chest. I intertwined my fingers in her fur, and she leaned against me, not taking her eyes off something standing a few feet to the right of the valkyrie.

The valkyrie smirked and said something too low for me to hear. A second later, a giant wolf appeared with ice-blue eyes.

Brilliant white wings were tucked in tightly against his sides. A few streaks of blood marred his perfect white coat.

"First the skogkatt and now the wolf." Nemain shook her head. "You really need to teach your companions how to greet friends when they come to visit."

"The last time I came to see you," the valkyrie said, "your grimalkin gave me bad luck for a week. I broke my favorite axe and fell into not one but *two* swamps. My hair was disgusting for days."

Nemain's gaze flitted up to the trees to where Jinx was no doubt hiding. *She gave that pathetic excuse for a cat the last piece of steak. That was MY steak,* he grumbled.

The valkyrie shrugged. "Didn't see your name on it."

"Why haven't you responded to any of my messages, Sigrun?" Nemain squared off against the valkyrie.

"I've been busy." Sigrun's dark brown eyes fell on me. "Besides, you know I stay out of valkyrie business."

"Just hear us out," Nemain said.

Elisa stepped away from me and shifted. After glaring one last time at the white wolf who was still looking at her like she was a juicy piece of steak, she moved to stand beside the other vampires.

Sigrun eyed them warily. "It wasn't bad enough that you brought some random valkyrie here, but you also had to bring along a bunch of vampire children?" I stiffened at how easily she dismissed my presence. Nemain believed Sigrun could help me, and I trusted her, so I bit my tongue. "You know I'm in hiding, yet you still brought a bunch of teeny bopper witnesses?"

"They're not going to tell anyone." When the valkyrie just stared at her, Nemain sighed. "Sigrun, let me introduce the teeny bopper vampires. Elisa, Misha, Damon, and Isabeau. All of them are Apex bloodlines and currently wanted by the Vampire Council. But I found them, so finders keepers."

All four vampires gave a little wave.

Sigrun said something under her breath that I was pretty sure was a prayer for patience.

"And this"—Nemain gestured at me and Finn—"is Brynhild. We all call her Bryn, because we're not assholes and she likes us." Nemain paused and glanced up at the trees once more. "Good point, Jinx. We are assholes. We're just not assholes to her. Most of the time."

Sigrun shifted her weight slightly, and her expression suggested she was rapidly losing patience with this long-winded introduction. Nemain's grin grew wider. "The little boy standing next to her is Finn. He's the son of the exiled fae king, Balor. Oh!" She snapped her fingers. "By the way, there's an exiled fae king named Balor. He created the devourers. Bryn and Finn are bonded, and they're both under my protection."

I refrained from slapping my hand across my face and I could see Elisa out of the corner of my eye trying to keep from doing the same. Maybe we should have brought Magos or Kaysea with us. They were both good at playing peacekeeper, whereas Nemain would see something on fire and take a perverse joy in throwing oil on it.

Nemain closed the distance between her and the valkyrie until she was standing directly in front of her. I had a couple inches on Nemain and was a little broader, but Nemain wasn't small by any definition. Sigrun towered over her, but the shifter didn't back down as her expression grew hard. "I had to join the Unseelie Court to protect them. I'm neck deep in shit between the fae, daemons, and devourers. So you're going to help Bryn figure out what the fuck it means to be a valkyrie, or I swear to the gods I will tell every loki in existence where you live. Hell, I'll open a gods damn gateway right outside your house. We'll see how much peace and quiet you get then."

Sigrun's nostrils flared as she stared Nemain down. My heart beat wildly, but I continued to keep my mouth shut.

Mostly because I had no idea what to say. This was not how I was expecting my first meeting with another valkyrie to go. Given that Sigrun hadn't leapt at the chance to meet me as soon as Nemain sent her a message informing her of my existence, I hadn't been expecting her to be super excited about meeting me. But I hadn't been expecting outright rejection either. An old pang stabbed at me as once again finding myself unwanted by a valkyrie.

Sigrun's fiery eyes looked at me. I had been a babe when my mother had abandoned me. But I was older now, and I wouldn't let Sigrun see me as weak. I raised my chin and met her stare. Something akin to weariness flashed across her face.

"I will give you three days, during which time you will help me find whatever new beastie is causing trouble in my realm. After that, you're all gone."

Chapter Five

THREE DAYS WASN'T enough time. I stared at the flames crackling in the fire outside Sigrun's cottage. We'd stayed there for the night, rather than return to our apartments to sleep. I was fairly certain Nemain was convinced if we left the realm, even for a few hours, Sigrun would pack up and leave. Normally the vampires would be up for at least a few more hours, but Sigrun had made it clear she wanted to get an early start in the morning. So Elisa was trying to convince Isabeau to go to sleep. Damon and Misha had already passed out and were snoring on the floor in front of the fireplace the last time I'd checked.

Luna and Jinx were curled up with Finn on a chair. He'd also had no problems going to sleep. I tossed a couple more logs into the fire pit. Elisa had sensed I needed some time to myself and had promised to keep an eye on Finn while she got Isabeau settled. Being in charge and responsible for others seemed to come so naturally to her.

Meanwhile, I felt adrift and constantly several steps behind everyone else.

The fae villages I'd grown up in had been remote and

rarely visited by the fae who lived outside the mountain range, let alone other species. A young sidhe girl I'd dated for a few months had taken me to the city at the base of the mountains, Cathair na Sneachta. I'd been overwhelmed by the amount of people and magic being thrown about, and she'd taken me to a quieter area. She hadn't minded about my freakout because we'd still been deeply in lust with each other at that stage of our relationship, so spending the afternoon exploring each other's bodies was more exciting than the city.

She'd also been the first one to take me outside the fae realm, carefully selecting a quiet daemon tavern that was rarely crowded. That had been my first time meeting a daemon. No other species had been there at the time.

Nemain was the first feline shifter I'd ever met, which, considering how few of them still existed, wasn't that surprising. Through her, I'd met vampires, werewolves, dragons, and a handful of other species. There was so much I didn't know. And I needed to learn it all to protect Finn. Nemain and the others could teach me most of it. But there was only one person who could teach me about my valkyrie magic. And she was only giving me three days.

I stared at the fire in frustration, trying to think of ways to change Sigrun's mind. I'd tried talking to her on the way back, but she'd shut down every attempt at conversation. She'd stormed off shortly after we'd gotten back, the wolf on her heels. None of us had seen Viggo, for which I was grateful. I didn't think I had it in me to deal with any more insults from the skogkatt. Nemain had gone after Sigrun and told me not to worry. Like that was possible.

Nemain was adamant we couldn't go to any other valkyries. She'd only given me vague answers as to why that wouldn't be a good idea. I had an inkling it had to do with Finn and my bonding with him. Based on how Viggo had reacted to it earlier, I suspected the other valkyries would react the same. But if Sigrun refused to help me, I'd have to try. When I'd felt my magic rising earlier, when Gunnar had attacked Elisa, I'd had no control over it. Some part of me knew I would never hurt Finn. Even accidentally, my magic would never target him. But if I'd harmed Elisa and the others, I would never have forgiven myself.

A glimmer of white in the dark caught my attention, and Gunnar emerged from the woods. He moved like a ghost, not a sound betraying his massive paws as he stalked across the clearing. I didn't say anything as he took up a position on the other side of the fire pit, settling down on his haunches with his mighty feathered wings folded against his sides. On equally quiet feet, Sigrun took a seat on a fallen log behind him, her eyes catching the light of the fire and casting a red glow.

"Where's Nemain?" I asked when the shifter didn't appear from the forest.

"She needs to burn off some steam," Sigrun said in a deep, measured tone. "These woods are good for that. She'll return in the morning."

"You know her that well?"

"I've known Nemain and all her secrets for a long time." The corners of the valkyrie's lips tilted upward slightly. "The secrets she knew about, anyway. I would have loved to have seen her face when she learned she was the daughter of The Morrigan and The Erlking." She chuckled. "And now Nemain, someone who has always hated the fae and their politics, is serving the Unseelie Queen herself."

My jaw hardened at the reminder of what Nemain had sacrificed to keep Finn safe.

Your fault, your fault, your fault, the voice inside my head chanted.

"Did Nemain tell you everything? About me and Finn? About the prophecy?"

Sigrun's eyes darkened as she stared at the flames between

us. "No good ever comes from listening to prophecies. They're all bullshit."

I sat up straighter, frowning at the fire. "I thought you would be more understanding about all this once you heard the prophecy. Aren't the Norns revered by the valkyries?"

"Listening to the prophetic nonsense of the Norns is what caused the fall of our realms," Sigrun snarled. "Ragnarok was bullshit."

"Wha—"

"It doesn't matter, and I will not speak of it. You and the boy are bonded and Nemain has joined the Unseelie Court. There is no undoing any of that."

"I need to know," I pushed. "You're only giving me three days, and that's not enough time to learn all the things I must know to protect Finn. I'll have no choice but to go to the other valkyries, so I need to know more of our history."

Sigrun let out a harsh laugh. "No valkyrie has ever bonded with a fae before. That alone would make them wary of you and unlikely to help you in any way. But if the Norns see that boy, they'll know who he is. What he is. They'll kill you both. They can't allow that bond to exist."

"Why? What about the bond between me and Finn would frighten them so much?"

"Nemain told me how you awakened your powers. For a valkyrie to come into our powers, we have to accept the death of our first life and the beginning of our second life. We cannot begin this second life without binding ourselves to another. The valkyries have bonded almost exclusively with the Aesir or Vanir. It is a deeply personal choice whom we choose to bond with. I don't have to tell you what it means." Sigrun's steely gaze fell on me, and I gave her a deep nod. Finn and I would be tied together for the rest of our lives. The bond was tethered into my soul, and with each day that passed, it grow stronger. "Your bond is in its infancy. Soon you'll be able to feel each other's emotions. You'll each have to practice control so you don't overwhelm the other." Sigrun paused. "It's also possible to draw power from each other."

"What do you mean?" I thought about my magic spiraling out of control earlier in the day and chewed on the inside of my cheek. If Finn started to feel my emotions soon, I couldn't let my panic rise like that again. I had to do better.

"We're born for war," Sigrun said. "Fighting is in our blood, and we look for that kinship with whomever we choose to bond. If you need more power in a fight, you can draw the raw magic from your bonded and funnel it into yourself for a boost. Your bonded can do the same. It's a delicate dance and requires absolute trust on both ends."

"What happens if you draw too much?"

"Whoever is pulling in the power would feel the other lessen and eventually pass out. Normally, at the first signs of that, they would stop because passing out on a battlefield results in death."

"Has anyone ever kept pulling?" I asked. "Even after their bonded passed out?"

"Doing so would be a deep betrayal of the bond," Sigrun said after a couple of heartbeats. "If a valkyrie dies, their bonded can usually survive the death, although it often destroys their mind. But it's generally understood that if the one bonded to a valkyrie dies, the valkyrie dies with them. This is not always true." Sigrun's eyes blazed a fiery red, and the air surrounding her felt charged as her power poured off her in waves. I flared my wings wide but stayed seated, baring my teeth against the display of power. Magic skittered across my skin, causing the hair on my arms to rise. Gunnar raised his head and let out a low grumble. Sigrun pulled her magic back, and her eyes faded back to their normal color. "It is possible to survive the death of our bonded, if that death is the result of us pulling their magic out of them and not stopping until every last drop is within us."

I recoiled, horror seeping into my bones. "You killed your bonded," I whispered. Revulsion swept through me, and I wished for a blade so I could bury it in Sigrun's heart. And Viggo had the audacity to call Finn an abomination. He had to know what Sigrun was, what she had done.

"Yes. And that expression on your face is the same one all the valkyries give me when they see me. Also, like you, they want to kill me for committing this atrocity." She smiled as she stared into the fire, and it was completely devoid of any emotion. Maybe this was why she moved like a ghost, because for all intents and purposes, she was one. I couldn't imagine living in a world without Finn, and I'd only been bonded to him for a few months.

"There's a reason I hate prophecies. The warrior I bonded with was honorable. He was powerful, but more importantly, he was a good person who wanted to do right by his people. I would have followed him anywhere. For a long time, I did. The prophecy surrounding Ragnarok caused a civil war throughout Yggdrasil. I never believed in it. I thought Ragnarok was rubbish. But my bonded believed in it wholeheartedly. He thought he was doing what was best for his people." Grief and anger cracked through Sigrun's hardened mask. "By the end, he was a person I didn't recognize. Someone who justified the slaughter of the innocent for what he thought was the greater good. Other valkyries were in similar situations, but they chose to stay with their bonded to the very end no matter the cost. I chose to walk a different path."

Sigrun fell silent, and I didn't respond. I didn't know what I could say to that. The idea of killing Finn shook me to my core. The prophecy surrounding Finn proclaimed he had the potential to fall to darkness and bring about the end of the realms. Given that his parents were responsible for the creation of the devourers that had caused numerous realms to fall and entire species to go extinct, Finn's dark destiny was worrisome. Nemain was supposed to keep Finn off that dark path, and I was determined to help her. But what if we failed? Could I kill Finn if it meant saving everyone else?

Just thinking about it caused my blood to run cold and my magic to shift nervously within me. "How did you survive it?" The words spilled out of me before I could think better of it.

Minutes ticked by and I thought Sigrun wouldn't answer. Gunnar rose to his feet and shook his wings loose. With a few long bounding leaps, he took to the sky. Sigrun rose and spread her golden wings wide. "Because I already died once, and as you will learn, valkyries are quite hard to kill once their power has awakened. I'm the most powerful valkyrie in existence. When the others learned what I had done, they tried to kill me." Sigrun scoffed. "They succeeded multiple times. But my soul is no longer welcome in Valhalla, and Hel won't accept it either. So every time I die, I awaken again. Believe me when I say it's not a pleasant experience.

"I just wish to be left alone now." The fire banked as Sigrun beat her wings and rose into the air. "I cannot be your mentor, young valkyrie, because I have nothing left to give."

AN HOUR later I was still sitting by the fire pit, watching the logs burn down to coals, trying to come to terms with what Sigrun had told me. Part of me had also hoped Nemain would return so I could yell at her for bringing me here. She must have known Sigrun's background given her history with the valkyrie. But Nemain never showed up and Sigrun didn't return.

The rational part of me understood why Sigrun did what she did, and how heartbreaking that choice must have been.

Finn was the child of two cruel and powerful megalomaniacs, and it was prophesied that he would bring about the destruction of the realms. But when I thought about…ending him… to save everyone else. The blood in my veins turned to ice.

No. Sigrun had chosen wrong. There must have been something else she could have done.

"How did it go?" Elisa asked softly from where she curled up on some blankets in the corner. From her vantage point, she could keep everyone in her view and see anyone entering the cottage from the front or back door. My eyes skimmed over the room quickly, seeing everyone in the same position as earlier. Isabeau had joined Finn on the oversized chair he'd fallen asleep on. Both of the grimalkins were nestled in with them.

Quietly, I walked across the room and took a seat next to Elisa on the floor, shuffling around until my wings were comfortable. "Not great," I admitted. "I think it might have been a mistake to come here."

"Why?" Elisa spread the blanket from her lap over both of us. I rubbed my face and leaned my head back against the wall, recounting my conversation with Sigrun.

"Now when I look at Sigrun, all I see is a valkyrie that killed her bonded."

"I imagine that's what most people see," Elisa murmured. "I admit I don't know much about Ragnarok. Most of the writings about it available in the human realm are just pretty versions with little truth in them. I do know it was a brutal civil war, and both sides committed horrible atrocities. It's been well over a thousand years and the realms of Yggdrasil are still recovering. Almost all the leaders on both sides perished in the final battles. They don't like to talk about it with outsiders. It sounds like Sigrun had to make an impossible choice and has been living with the consequence ever since."

"She betrayed her bonded," I snarled, causing Finn to stir slightly. I took a deep breath and lowered my voice. "The bond . . . it's like a living thing. The one between me and Finn is growing stronger every day. To use that bond to kill the other is unforgivable."

"Maybe her bonded betrayed her first."

My head snapped to the side as I stared at Elisa. "How can you say that?"

Elisa pursed her lips and gazed at the fire crackling in front of Misha and Damon. "There was another in our group in the beginning. An older girl, the original leader of our little family unit. Katrina."

"You've never mentioned her," I said slowly.

"No one knows about her but me, Damon, and Misha," Elisa said tightly. "The Council usually kept us together in groups of four or six."

"Easy to divide." I nodded, my mind naturally thinking about how this would work well in a fight or on a mission. "You can split up into pairs or fight as a group. Altogether, the group is still small enough that you would know each other well and be able to play on each other's strengths and weaknesses."

"Exactly. We have always been a group of four, but Katrina was our leader in the beginning. She was two years older than me and everything you would want in an older sister." Her jaw was hard set and her shoulders tense like I'd never seen in her before, even when she was annoyed at Misha or frustrated with Isabeau. I started to reach my hand towards her but stopped, unsure if Elisa wanted to be touched right then.

"She was fiercely protective of us, and we loved her for it. Our devotion to her was absolute, and even though we knew we couldn't trust the Council, we trusted her. Even when she started spending more time away from us and with the Council members. We—I assumed she was just going along with it to protect us. Looking back, there were signs we should have seen. But none of us wanted to."

"What was her power?" I asked curiously. Vampires never

came to the fae realms and after meeting Elisa and the others, I found their different types of magic fascinating.

"Compulsion," Elisa practically spat.

"Mind control?" I didn't bother keeping the disgust out of my voice. Telepathic abilities among the fae were rare. Their relationship with magic was incredibly powerful, but mostly rooted in nature. The more powerful fae could also manipulate raw magic, but anything beyond basic telepathy was almost unheard of. I'd heard rumors some daemons had strong psychic skills and could weave illusions so vivid and real, you'd never know it wasn't. The thought of someone being able to trick you like that horrified me. But not as much as someone who could control your mind and make you do unspeakable things.

"It's one of the more prolific bloodlines among the Apex vampires. Even weak compulsion works well against were-wolves. They're surprisingly susceptible to most magic. Katrina was strong and was the answer to the question the Council had been asking themselves for years. How do you get unquestion-able loyalty from your soldiers?"

I stilled, a chill spreading through me. "They wanted to use compulsion on all of you."

Elisa swallowed once and gave me a shallow nod. This had to have happened a long time ago because it was before Isabeau had joined them. But the look of devastation and betrayal on her face was still so raw, and so similar to what I had seen on Sigrun's face earlier. I shifted forward slightly and tentatively spread my wings. Elisa leaned forward so my wing could slide behind her. Her warm body leaned against me, and I wrapped my wings around us both.

Leaning her head on my shoulder, she continued. "Some-where along the way, Katrina had become a true believer in the war against the werewolves. The Council had arranged to take her to places where the wolves had attacked vampires.

Slaughtered vampire children. I'm not defending what the wolves did. They committed plenty of atrocities in this war, but the Council no doubt only showed Katrina what they wanted her to see. I don't understand why she fell for that. She was so smart, she had to know they were manipulating her." Elisa paused, and I didn't push, letting her take her time in this. "The three of us were coming into our magic, and our training had been progressing well. The Council wanted to send us out into the field, but not without a leash."

"They asked Katrina to use compulsion on you?" My voice hitched. "And she agreed to that?"

"She didn't think it was necessary because she thought we would follow her anywhere. But at that point, we'd started to notice the changes in her. She wanted us to go along with the compulsion, because in her mind it's what we would have wanted to do anyway, so what did it matter if her magic was cementing that need in place? I tried to explain we had no interest in fighting against the werewolves, and she acted like I'd struck her. Before I could reason with her more, she lashed out with her magic." Elisa went rigid against me, and I wrapped my hand around hers. She squeezed back, and my wings pulled her in closer.

"I felt my will leaving my body. Everything became fuzzy, but before I lost myself, the wolf took over." Elisa's words were barely above a whisper. "When I came back to my senses, blood was running down my throat. Her blood. I shifted back and tried to stop the bleeding, but half of her throat was gone."

"Did she die?" If she was still alive I felt the overwhelming need to hunt her down and neutralize the threat. Even if my crush on Elisa never went beyond that, she was still my friend. And this other vampire had hurt her. My magic stirred within me sensing my bloodlust.

"I don't know." Elisa went silent for a couple of minutes,

studying our intertwined hands. "I told the Council guards that I didn't know what happened. I thought they would kill me, but they decided my wolf nature had a bad reaction to the compulsion and they would have to be more careful about using it on those of us with more animalistic tendencies. I don't know if they used it on others, but they never tried on our group again.

"Katrina had grown up with us. She'd been through the same hell, and we trusted her with our lives. She didn't see using compulsion on us as a betrayal." Elisa pulled back enough to meet my eyes. "I did what I had to do to protect myself and the others, but I will also carry the guilt of what I did to Katrina with me for the rest of my life. We betrayed each other, and those are difficult wounds to heal. You should give Sigrun a chance."

My immediate response was to say that what Elisa had gone through was different. But was it really? Or was I just oversimplifying a complicated issue to avoid thinking about a hard choice I might have to make in the future?

"Thank you for sharing this with me. I'll try to keep an open mind with Sigrun."

"Good, that's all I want you to do." Elisa leaned her head back on my shoulder, and I kissed the top of her head without thinking. I froze, thinking I'd gone too far, but Elisa burrowed in deeper against me.

"Stop overthinking things, valkyrie. You already bonded with the fae child of an exiled king. You might as well have a vampire girlfriend, too."

I let out a breathy laugh and leaned my head against hers, not wanting to break the spell she was putting me under. The cracking sound of the fire gradually lulled us both to sleep.

Chapter Six

THE SOUND of the door creaking open in the early hours before sunrise woke me and most of the vampires. Damon and Misha snapped their heads towards Isabeau, twin expressions of horror stamped on their faces, checking to see if the young girl had been woken by the noise. Relief flickered in their eyes as they saw that she was still out cold, and they rolled over, promptly falling back asleep. Elisa snorted from where she was still tucked in against me. At some point in the night we'd changed positions so we could lie down, and her back was against my chest, my left wing draped over her.

Nemain smirked at us as she made her way over.

"Don't start, you cat-eyed devil," Elisa grumbled and pulled a pillow over her head. I propped myself up on my elbow and stared down at her wide-eyed and looked back up at Nemain.

"I hope you're not a morning person, because Elisa is most definitely not."

Elisa raised her hand and flipped Nemain off, letting it thump back to the floor. A low chuckle tumbled out of Nemain's lips, and she jerked her head towards the door. "Let's go check in with Sigrun. We'll give the vamp brats another hour of sleep."

I carefully untangled myself from Elisa, who let out a few choice swear words, most of which I didn't understand. Nemain tossed me an extra blanket, and I draped it over the sleeping vampire and followed Nemain outside.

The crisp morning air felt good against my skin as I gazed out over the meadow. The sun was still another thirty minutes or so from rising, but the sky was already lightening and the critters who lived in the tall grass were awake. Flocks of small birds flittered around, snapping insects out of the air, while several large lizards made their way up the few rocky outcroppings in preparation for basking.

"I can see why she likes it here," I said. "It's peaceful."

Nemain moved to stand next to me. She looked out across the tall grassy meadow with a wistful and slightly melancholic expression. "I think this is what Kanima was like."

"Kanima?"

"The home realm of the feline shifters. Endless grassy plains stretched across the middle of the realm before giving way to the deep jungles of the south."

I'd never even heard of the realm before, but then I could barely name all the fae realms. I'd never planned on leaving the mountains, so I didn't have a reason to learn about other realms. I glanced at Nemain. "Have you ever tried to go back?"

"Only once." Nemain's lips thinned into a hard line. "The devourers must have found a food source to sustain them because they're still there, and they're very aggressive. I'd need a small army to go back and explore it, and a massive one to take it back from them, and there's no reason to. I was born in the human realm. Kanima is not my home."

"I'm sorry."

Nemain shrugged.

Deciding we needed to address this before going any further, I asked her what was really on my mind. "Sigrun told me about what happened to her bonded. Why didn't you tell me?"

"It wasn't my story to tell." She slid her emerald green eyes towards me. "Plus, I figured you'd be horrified at the idea of a valkyrie killing their bonded and would have refused to speak with her."

I looked away from her before admitting how I had felt. "I was ready to go home after she told me last night."

"But then Elisa told you about Katrina, and now you're having a harder time painting Sigrun's decision as a monstrous one that you would never make. It's easy to say you would never do such a thing when you've never been in that position. Sometimes there are no good options. But life still forces you to pick one."

"You know about Katrina?" I blinked in surprise.

"The vamp kids sometimes forget who I am and what I'm capable of," Nemain said wryly. "I've survived the last few centuries because I make it a point to know everything about enemies and my allies. I've been digging into the Vampire Council as soon as they joined forces with the warlocks, and when Elisa and the others moved in. Mikhail might be an annoying asshat, but he did serve the Council for a long time and learned many of their secrets along the way. He remembers when they were experimenting with compulsion, and he heard about the incident with Elisa and Katrina."

"Does he know if Katrina is still alive?" I asked. My heart started beating rapidly as my magic rose. One single thought bounced around in my mind. *Destroy the threat.*

"No." Nemain shook her head. "If we discovered she was alive, I would let Elisa and the others know because they have a right to know that. And it's something we'd have to prepare for.

Until then, I don't push Elisa to talk about what they went through while they were under the Council's thumb."

I frowned, not liking the idea that such a powerful enemy was out there somewhere. Nemain likely didn't view her or the Vampire Council as much of a threat, given all the enemies gunning for her. I didn't like it though. Maybe I could talk to Mikhail about it when we got home.

The sound of metal rhythmically clanging against metal pulled me from my thoughts. Nemain looked towards the workshop behind the cottage. "Come on, let's go see what Sigrun is up to."

I followed Nemain around back, curiosity rising as we approached the large double doors that had been thrown open. I still felt conflicted about what Sigrun had told me about her past, but I had promised Elisa that I would keep an open mind. Sigrun held a hammer in one hand as she studied a glowing piece of metal lying on an anvil. Sweat glistened across her dark skin as she tilted her head to the side, pondering the weapon she was working on. Her waist length braids had been clipped back away from her face.

"A sword?" I asked, surprised as Nemain and I stood a safe distance away. Most of the weapons hanging inside the cottage were axes and hammers, with the occasional spear. The axe Sigrun had carried yesterday was hanging on a hook by the doors.

Nemain's eyes lit up, and she stepped forward. "Are you finally making me a sword?"

Sigrun grunted. "Not if you keep talking to me."

Nemain rolled her eyes but took a few steps back to study all the shields hanging on the wall. Sigrun went back to striking the sword, and my eyes drifted to the wall behind her. Like the wall Nemain was standing in front of, shields mostly lined this one. Without realizing it, I stepped forward until I was mere inches away and ran my fingers across the exquisite detailing on one of them. They looked like they were made of pure silver with gold designs, but I knew that couldn't be the case, since neither of those minerals would be strong enough to serve as a shield. Maybe if they were magicked?

I didn't feel any magic off them, but that didn't mean it wasn't there. Maybe it had to be activated somehow. Or perhaps the shields were made of material I wasn't familiar with. I'd never seen anyone fight with a shield before. Most of the fae in the villages I'd grown up in relied on magic, and Nemain usually dual-wielded her swords. These shields were massive and had to be quite heavy, which would make them slow. But something about them called to me.

"Pick one," Sigrun said as she raised the sword in the air, studying it. After a few seconds, she took it to a large container of silvery water and shoved the sword in. Steam rose in the air along with wisps of light. Sigrun pulled the sword free, and it glowed briefly. Faint blue runes shone down its side and faded into the blade. The valkyrie tossed the sword to Nemain as if it were nothing. Nemain snatched it out of the air and stared at it the same way she stared at a plate full of bacon. "Go drool over it somewhere else," Sigrun said, a faint smile tugging at her lips.

Nemain nodded and walked out of the workshop, twirling the blade in a few practiced moves as if getting used to the size and weight. Turning back to me, Sigrun nodded at the wall of shields again. "Pick one."

"These are too nice for me." I shook my head and stepped away from the wall. "Besides, I don't know how to fight with a shield and don't have anyone to teach me."

"Nemain prefers swords, but she can still teach you the basics of using a shield and axe. That good-looking vampire living with her knows his way around a shield and axe as well."

I snorted. "You'll have to be more specific about the

vampire. Pretty sure both Magos and Mikhail qualify as 'good-looking,' if that's your thing."

"Not all of us prefer lithe dark-haired beauties with sharp minds and tongues." Sigrun shrugged. "Good choice though. I can see why you like her."

"Not going to lecture me about becoming involved with a vampire? It doesn't go against some valkyrie code of conduct?"

Sigrun arched an eyebrow at me and walked over to the one wall that had weapons instead of shields. She pulled an axe off and tossed it back and forth in her hands before hanging it back on the wall. "It's truly amazing how Nemain turns everyone in her life into a smartass. You've been with her for what, a few months, and you're already becoming the valkyrie version of her."

"There are worse things to be."

She grunted, eyes scanning the various weapons. "I was referring to the more broadly built vampire. The one who looks like he could stop a dire wolf in its tracks."

"Magos," I said with a grin. "He also uses a sword."

Sigrun selected another axe and, after considering it for a moment, tossed it to me. I caught it awkwardly and held it out. It was heavy but manageable. "You should train with swords so you're familiar with how they're used in a fight, but they are not the weapon for you."

"Why not?" I tentatively swung the axe a few times, trying to get used to the feel. "I'm already familiar with sword fighting, and I've been practicing with Nemain the past few weeks. I'm improving quickly."

"Nemain prefers swords and daggers because she's fast. Same with the vampires. You will never match their speed, nor that of many other beings. We are strong, not fast. You will not parry. You will not defeat your enemies by slowly picking them apart." Sigrun pulled a well-worn axe off the wall and walked over to a wooden practice dummy that had clearly already taken some hard hits. Deep grooves were scattered across the body, in some places large chunks were missing entirely. In one swift practiced move, she pulled the axe back and swung it forward. The top half of the dummy fell to the ground. "You will break them and move on to the next."

I felt the weight of the axe more acutely in my hand and I frowned at it before studying the shields on the wall. "The axes require two hands to wield properly. How do you use the shield?"

Sigrun raised her right arm towards me, revealing a wide silver band around her wrist with thin golden lines. In a blink, a shield popped into existence, covering most of her body before shrinking back down to the bracelet. "You will need to practice," she said. "Raising the shield needs to happen without thought when you're in battle."

"I don't have any money," I said quietly. "The little I had, I left behind in the fae realms."

"I have no need of your money. As you can see, I have no shortage of shields and blades. When you live as long as I have, you have a tendency to collect a lot of weapons along the way. Plus I enjoy the process of making them. I'm not as skilled as the dwarves but I find that it calms my mind and keeps my skills sharp."

My gaze roamed over the wall until it snagged on one I couldn't look away from. "That one. I'll take that one."

***

"QUIT THAT!" Damon snapped after Elisa nipped at him again before diving back into the underbrush. Gunnar bounded after her. Apparently they'd worked out their wolfy issues because they'd been alternating between playing and tormenting Damon and Misha all morning, much to Isabeau's delight.

We'd taken a slightly different path this morning to explore another area of the forest. This section had a lot more vines and thick thorny bushes lining the space between the trees. The path we were on was well-worn, and I hoped we wouldn't have to venture off it. I eyed a pale green vine wrapped around a tree trunk, its thorns tipped a deep blood red. The axe on my back was a newly weighted presence, but I was already getting used to it. It felt like it belonged there. Nemain had rolled her eyes when she saw it and made some comment about valkyries and their bloody axes and hammers. I hadn't shown anyone the shield yet. It felt right when I chose it, but a warm thread of embarrassment ran through me at the thought of showing it to Elisa.

"He's just enjoying having another wolf to play with," Sigrun said from where she and Nemain walked ahead of everyone. "The wolves of Niflheim live in packs, but he's been with me since he was a pup."

"What happened to his pack?" I asked.

"Nidhogg," Sigrun said grimly. "It was shortly after Ragnarok started. Odin unleashed her, but the fool couldn't control her. She tore through the realms, decimating everything in her path before she was finally contained. Gunnar's pack was a casualty of that."

"Who or what is Nidhogg?" Misha teleported a few steps behind Sigrun and Nemain, leaving Damon to fend off the wolves on his own.

"A dragon . . . sort of," Nemain said.

"Like Eddie?" Isabeau perked up.

We all groaned. Dragons were thought to be extinct. The story of them was well-known, even to folks like me who had grown up in the middle of nowhere. The daemons and dragons shared the same home realm, and for most of their lives, the daemons had been hunted down and tormented by the dragons. They'd managed to escape the realm, and when they grew in power and status, they took their revenge: locking the dragons in their home realm while ripping open gateways to realms full of devourers. The dragons had nowhere to go, and no one would help them because no one was willing to piss off the daemons at that point.

The cautionary tale was still whispered around campfires. The sidhe might technically be the most powerful in terms of magic. But the daemons were calculating and patient. And they did not forget or forgive those who crossed them. Everyone assumed the dragons had perished, but as it turns out, they'd been clinging to survival in their realm all this time. Eddie was a dragon who had been exiled from his realm. Apparently, that was what the dragon leadership did to those who opposed them. It was usually a death sentence since the daemons would brutally murder any dragon that managed to get free of the realm. But Eddie had survived, and we were all keeping that on the down low.

Or at least we were trying to.

"Isabeau," Misha warned. "We've talked about this, remember?"

The young vampire girl giggled and skipped ahead, tugging Finn along with her. Nemain glanced at Luna and Jinx, and both grimalkins bounded after the children. *We should leave her here,* Jinx grumbled.

"You will do no such thing," Sigrun growled. "Viggo is still sulking somewhere after whatever she did to him yesterday."

"Do we know . . . what she did?" I asked quietly. Not that it mattered. We already knew Isabeau could read our thoughts with ridiculous ease. It was how she knew Eddie was a dragon before any of us told her. She seemed to have a little trouble reading Eddie's mind, which was probably the only reason she hadn't learned his secret earlier. But Eddie was a powerful telepath. The rest of us stood no chance against her.

No, Elisa said from where she slunk through the brush. I couldn't see her, but I felt her presence. *I tried to talk to her about it, but she wouldn't tell me. I got the impression she was scared about what she'd done. I don't think she's ever done that before.*

"Is there anything we can do?" I asked. Isabeau was a terror, but I liked her. Plus she was fiercely protective of Finn, which in turn made me protective of her.

We just have to keep doing what we've been doing, Elisa replied. *When our magic first starts to manifest, it tends to happen in spurts. Control is dodgy for the first couple of years. I was once stuck as a wolf for three weeks.*

"That was hilarious." Misha chuckled. Elisa shot out of the brush without warning and bit his thigh before leaping back into the underbrush. "You bitch!" He snarled, vanishing in an instant. Curses and growls rose in the woods around us as the two vampires battled each other.

Sigrun let out a long-suffering sigh. "You know, I like this realm because it's quiet." She glared at Nemain. "Not full of loud, obnoxious vampire children. I don't know how you live with this every day."

"Whiskey," Nemain said automatically, getting a chuckle out of me.

"I'm surprised you don't live somewhere like this, Nemain," Damon said. "I mean . . . you don't like people, and there are lots of woods for you run around in here."

She likes sushi too much, Jinx said from somewhere up in the trees. *And ceviche. Human food in general, especially anything fish related.*

"Couldn't you just learn to make that, though?" Damon frowned.

A deep rumbling laugh poured out of Jinx, and some of the branches shook. *Nemain? Cook?* The branch shook harder. *She tried to make a grilled cheese sandwich last week and set the kitchen on fire.*

"I did not!" Nemain snarled. "Only the pan caught on fire!"

Finn glanced up in the trees where Jinx was still laughing and then over his shoulder at Nemain. "Is that why you always order us pizza?"

"I'm going to scout ahead," Nemain said evenly and took off at a fast jog. Elisa and Gunnar leapt out from the sides of the trail and bounded after her.

"Is it always like this?" Sigrun asked.

"No," I replied with a grin. "It's even worse when Mikhail's here."

Chapter Seven

WE WALKED for another hour before we joined up with
Nemain again. She was crouched on a rocky overhang with
Elisa on one side and Gunnar on the other. All three had a
predatory stillness to them as they watched something below.
Even Isabeau quieted as we approached them, her vampire
nature rising as the usually loud girl moved with a silent preter-
natural grace. Misha and Damon moved to guard Finn and
Isabeau, and we all looked over the edge to see what had
captured the attention of Nemain and the wolves.

"Meindyr," I said quietly. The small furry creatures were
pacing in front of a large cave entrance. Several broken bodies
were scattered in the small field in front of the cave. The
meindyr had found prey in the area and had dragged it back
here. Unlike most predators that would have made the most
out of whatever they caught; the animals left in the meadow
had chunks torn out of them but were mostly whole. My
stomach churned. I understood the nature of things. Some
beings must die for others to live. But this was such a waste,
and I knew the creatures stretched out before me hadn't gone
easily. Nothing about their deaths had been quick.

I counted the agitated furry bodies that scurried around beneath us. They moved fast, and the dried grass in front of the cave concealed their movements, but I thought there were at least forty of them. At first glance they didn't look all that intimidating, but I had once wandered into a swamp full of boggarts, so I was all too aware of how quickly one could be overwhelmed by small beings with sharp teeth and claws.

"They're agitated," Nemain said. "Something in that cave has them all riled up."

Sigrun pursed her lips. "We should get them cleared out then so we can investigate." She surveyed me and the vampires. "How well have you trained them?"

A wild grin spread across Nemain's face. "Let's find out."

"What?" Misha asked, eyebrows bunching together. Before he could react, Nemain took a step back and shoved him and Damon off the ledge. It was only a twenty-foot drop to the floor of the clearing, and they both managed to land on their feet.

The black wolf swung its head up and growled at Nemain before leaping down to join the others.

Nemain pulled her twin swords free. "Boys!" Damon and Misha glared up at Nemain, and she tossed the swords down. They caught them and turned to face the meindyr who had just sensed something else had joined them in the clearing. "Consider this a training exercise! Remember your lessons!" Nemain shouted. "Whoever kills the most is off Isabeau babysitting duties for a week!"

The teenage vampire boys looked at each other and bellowed as they raised their swords and launched themselves at the encroaching meindyr. Isabeau leapt forward, but Nemain snatched her out of the air. "I don't think so, little one." Isabeau hissed and tried to pull free, but Nemain's hold didn't slip. "If you don't behave, I'll open a gateway and toss your ass back in the apartment."

The young vampire stuck out her bottom lip in a pout and plopped down. Nemain sat down beside her, wrapping an arm around her shoulders. After a moment, Finn sat next to Isabeau and the grimalkins settled in place next to him.

"Is this safe?" I chewed on my lip a I watched the vampires hack at the meindyr. The little devourers were fast and there were so many of them...

"Safe enough." Nemain shrugged.

I stared at her, and one corner of her mouth tugged up into a lopsided grin.

"We won't let any serious harm come to any of you." It did not escape my notice her inclusion of the word serious. Nemain's smile twisted and her expression turned grave. "The world is a dangerous place. I'm doing everything I can to help all of you prepare for it, but sparring in the safety of our apartment only goes so far. This is a rare opportunity for all of you to get some experience against devourers in a situation where your lives aren't at risk."

Two meindyr launched themselves at Damon, aiming for his throat. He jumped back but not fast enough. Even from here I could see the long claws of one of the meindyr slice into his shoulder. I winced as blood poured from the wound. But Damon recovered quickly, his sword slicing through the devourer when it dropped to the ground. I hated to see my friends hurt, but I knew Nemain was right. We didn't have the luxury of living sheltered lives.

I felt Sigrun's gaze on me and looked at her. "Go try out the shield and axe." She gestured towards the others. "We can adjust as necessary afterwards, and I'll tell Nemain moves that will be good for you to practice."

It took a couple of tries, but I managed to pull the axe free from the hook strapped to my back with a leather harness. Snapping my wings open, I leapt into the air, surveying the battle taking place below me. Damon and Misha were fighting back to back, cutting down every meindyr that lunged towards them. Elisa was moving in a steady circle around them, stirring up the small devourers. She never stayed still long enough for them to concentrate on her, instead driving them towards the other two vampires. They clearly had a system down and were executing it well. Damon was likely using his magic to ensure they could all communicate telepathically, but either he wasn't looping me in on purpose or he couldn't reach me. Which meant I was on my own.

Another wave of devourers poured out of the cave mouth, and I dove towards them. My knees shook as I hit the ground. I really needed to work on my landings. The meindyr focused on me and launched themselves from all directions. The shield flared to life from my wrist, but my back was exposed, and I let out a hiss of pain as several devourers latched onto my wings. The shield vanished, and more leapt towards me. I clumsily swung my axe and knocked a bunch of them away. The axe was so much heavier than the swords I'd been practicing with, and the meindyr were so light that my swings were too strong. Every time my concentration slipped, the shield would disappear.

"This is an awful fighting strategy," I growled. Pain flared in my wings as more devourers bit down.

"You're not a delicate princess!" Sigrun bellowed. "Your wings won't break. Why are you just standing there?"

"You're a terrible teacher!" I screamed.

"Maybe you're just not asking the right questions," Sigrun retorted.

Another meindyr dug its claws and fangs into me. I yanked it off and stomped on it. Two more quickly took its place.

"GET THE FUCK OFF ME!" I pulled my wings in tight and then snapped them open as I pushed upwards. Magic flared within me, and I spun in place for a few seconds. The meindyr that had been clinging to my wings fell back, slamming into the ground, and golden feathers flew after them, impaling the furry bodies to the ground. *What the hell?*

I drew my wings in closer, running my hands along the edges. They felt fine. Before I could think more about how I had flung feathered spears from my wings, more meindyr attacked. I raised my arm, and the shield flared to life. The small devourers bounced off it. Lowering my arm, I let the shield fall away and swung my axe, cutting through three furry bodies. I spun as I saw two leap out of the corner of my eye and brought the shield back up, but not quickly enough. One was deflected, but the other made it through my guard, its curved claws slicing into my flesh. I screamed as it bit down and tore a mouthful of flesh away. Three more attacked from the other side and bit down on my leg. I slammed the shield back, knocking them off my leg, but the wounds felt cold, and with every bite, my magic and energy waned.

More tried to swarm me, and I frantically knocked them back. For every two that fell to my axe, another three took their place. The vampires were being similarly swarmed but seemed to be handling it better. But if I tried to join them, I would only mess up their strategy. I gritted my teeth as I continued blocking with my shield and swinging my axe. The meindyr broke through my defenses and stole bits of flesh and magic. Fatigue plagued me.

I glanced up to the ledge where Nemain and Sigrun still stood, showing no signs of joining the fight. Finn looked worried, but he made no move to help me either. And I didn't want him to help me, damn it. I was supposed to be protecting him, not the other way around. I whirled, taking out another dozen meindyr. Where the fuck were they all coming from? I tried to summon the feathers that had flown out of my wings before, but it didn't work. I didn't know if that was because my magic was running low or if they were actual feathers I needed to regrow. So far, I was not all that impressed with Sigrun's teaching strategy.

"Any reason you're sticking to the ground, valkyrie?" Sigrun called out.

Because I'm an idiot who forgot I could fly.

I leapt upwards as another two dozen meindyr came running out of the cave, their three-inch long claws extended as they jumped after me. I rose a little higher to keep out of their reach, and they circled the ground beneath me, waiting for me to land. Much of the grass had been trampled down in our fight, but patches of it were long enough that I couldn't see them in it. As soon as I landed, they would swarm me again, but if I didn't land soon, they would overwhelm the vampires.

I knew Nemain and Sigrun wouldn't let any harm come to us. The wound on my side pulsed in pain, and I grimaced. No major harm, anyway. But I didn't want to need their help, and I had no doubt Elisa and the others felt the same.

Still . . . I felt like there was more to this lesson than just seeing how I handled myself in a fight. I studied the fight below as I pondered what I was missing. *Maybe you're just not asking the right questions.* I wasn't asking any questions. Oh. *Oh.*

I turned to face Sigrun. "Would you be willing to offer advice on the best strategy for fighting these creatures since you have experience with them?"

Both Nemain and Sigrun smiled widely. "Of course," Sigrun said. "What have you observed so far?"

"They're easy to kill," I said. "But they use their numbers to their advantage by attacking in swarms. Because of their small size, it's difficult to target them efficiently and they scatter when I go after them."

"On your own, they would be annoying to deal with, not dangerous necessarily, but it would be tedious to take them all out." Sigrun gestured to where the vampires were holding their own. "But you are not alone, and one of you can teleport. You need to draw them out and get them to focus on one person, then the rest of you can surround them. It'll be like. . ." Sigrun turned to Nemain. "What's that human expression?"

"Shooting fish in a barrel." Nemain grinned wickedly.

An idea formed in my mind, and I flew down and hovered above the vampires. "I have an idea!" I shouted.

"That would be great because my arm is getting tired!" Misha shouted.

"Damon and Elisa, you need to get out of here, jump up on the ledge or something. Just remove yourselves from this immediate area. Misha, I need you to stir them up. Teleport around in front of the cave, draw them out as much as possible. Once they're concentrated on you and their true numbers are out, we can surround all of them."

"I kind of hate this plan," Misha growled. "But I'm in."

Damon clapped a hand over Misha's shoulder and sprinted away. He tossed the sword back to Nemain and scrambled up the slippery slope to join her and the others. Elisa bounded after him, but the meindyr cut her off, not happy about their prey trying to escape. She nimbly avoided them and raced away in the other direction. The meindyr split into two groups, one concentrated on Misha and the other trailing after Elisa.

"Damn it," I swore and dove down. "To me, Elisa!" I flew in front of her and whirled around. The black wolf leapt up from the pack of meindyr closing in on her and shifted midair. Her body crashed against mine and she flung her arms around my neck. I grunted as I gripped her tight against me. "We'll have to practice this maneuver," I breathed.

"Agreed," she huffed, wrapping her legs around my waist. She pulled away from me enough to meet my gaze. "I can think of all kinds of reasons this position could be useful."

Heat rushed through me. "You are really distracting. You know that, right?"

She grinned. "You weren't getting the discreet suggestions I was giving you, so I figured a more direct approach was appropriate."

I shook my head ruefully. "You are trouble."

"The fun kind of trouble." She arched an eyebrow at me, and I laughed despite the pain still pulsing from my side.

I flew her towards the others, and she dropped off me, nimbly landing on her feet. I hovered in the air as we watched Misha teleport around in front of the cave. He made sure to spend enough time in certain spaces to draw out more of the meindyr before disappearing. After repeating the maneuver a dozen times, he took off running away from the cave.

"Now would be a great time to join me!" he shouted.

"Let's go!" I dove off the cliff and trusted Elisa and Damon to follow after me. Misha halted his breakneck pace for a moment, allowing the meindyr to catch up to him as we entered the fray. He teleported away to join us on the perimeter and immediately started cutting into the devourers. The meindyr had nowhere to go as we methodically cut through them.

My axe split a meindyr in two as it leapt towards me. I waited with my shield, but no more came forward. My eyes scanned the clearing, but nothing was moving except us, and no more devourers came out of the cave. Either we'd gotten all of them, or the remaining ones had scattered.

Elisa's dark blue eyes skimmed across the space, searching for any potential threats, and her eyes fell on my shield. She stared at the stylized wolf engraved with gold and slowly raised her eyes to meet mine. "I like your shield."

NEMAIN NIMBLY LEAPT down to the clearing and gestured at Finn and Isabeau. My heart clenched when Finn took a step off the cliff, but Nemain caught him easily, setting him down quickly so she could jump back a few paces to catch Isabeau who had decided to leap off. Elisa stiffened in alarm before letting her shoulders sag. We looked at each other and smiled faintly.

Sigrun landed next to me, and I forced myself to not take a step back. I still wasn't used to how imposing she was. It wasn't just her size, a fierceness about her gripped you and refused to let go. If Nemain was the blade cutting silently through the night, Sigrun was a blazing sword, holding back an army.

"Always make use of the resources available to you," she said. "There is no reason to rush into battle. Gather information first. Learn everything you can about your enemies so you can exploit their weaknesses."

"What if they don't have any weaknesses?"

"Then block them from accessing their strengths."

I nodded and tried to mimic the move I'd see Sigrun do so many times. I swung my axe behind me to return it to the hook between my wings . . . and missed. Pain lashed through me as the axe cut through the feathers into muscle, and I flinched.

"Go slower," Sigrun said, twisting her axe free in a practiced but slow motion and then setting it back on the hook. "Eventually you'll be able to do it without thinking, just as you will be able to draw the shield on instinct. There is no rushing this. It will take time and practice."

I didn't have time, I thought grimly. Finn's enemies would be coming after him now. With slow, jerky movements, I got the axe in its place between my wings and started to head towards Finn.

Sigrun placed a hand on my shoulder, stopping me in my tracks. "Use the resources available to you. You are not solely responsible for looking after the boy, and it would be foolish of you to attempt to do so all on your own. You have Nemain and those two vampire warriors at your disposal. Not to mention both Kaysea and Pele are invested in this boy's future and, therefore, in yours. All of them can aid in training you and protecting the boy in the meantime. *Use your resources.*"

"But not you, right?" I squared my shoulders as I arched an eyebrow at her. "Because the clock is ticking on the three days you gave me. No one else will be able to train me the way you can. Of all those resources you mentioned, who among them can explain my valkyrie magic? Who can tell me how to fling my wing feathers as if they're spears? Who can tell me how to vanish and hide my presence? Who can teach me how to shred minds and lay waste to armies? Who, Sigrun?" I took a step closer until only inches separated us. "Who, if not *you*?"

Her nostrils flared, and her eyes glowed red for a second before she brushed past me and headed towards the cave mouth. I stood there, rooted in place as rage and frustration warred within me. A small hand slipped into mine, and I blinked down at Finn. The green that ringed his golden eyes seemed brighter today. He squeezed my hand, and I let out a deep breath, letting go of the anger. It would do me no good.

I nodded gratefully at him, and we walked, hand in hand, toward the cave mouth where the others had gathered. Nemain and the vampires had their hands clamped over their noses and mouths as they studied whatever was inside. A slightly sweet, rotting smell hit me a second later, and my stomach turned. If it was hitting me this strongly, it must be hell on their senses.

Meindyr and other animals lay scattered across the cave. It was impossible to count them because they were all in pieces. I crouched near the body of a large deer like creature. Something had torn it's head almost all the way off and it was missing large chunks of flesh. Most of the injuries looked more like tears, it had been pulled apart rather than cut apart. Grimacing I leaned closer at a small cluster of wounds near it's neck. Bite marks. But not like the ones I'd seen Nemain leave behind in her feline form. These ones were small as if whatever left them didn't have large fangs for ripping.

"What did this?" I asked. "These wounds don't look like something a meindyr would leave."

"No." Sigrun shook her head. "They're not strong enough to do something like this, and it isn't how they feed, anyway. This is something else. . ." She looked deeper into the cave.

"Where does this lead?" Nemain asked.

"Out to the coast," Sigrun said absently. "We explored it when we first moved to this realm. After a quarter mile, there is a steep drop-off, and the rest of the caverns continue underground before opening into the cliff side. There's no way out once you go in, other than backtracking or continuing forward."

Nemain grimaced. "That's less than ideal."

Viggo popped into existence next to the shredded meindyr, and all of us jumped, except Nemain and Sigrun. Nemain eyed the skogkatt sharply. "You smell like a dog."

Gunnar raised his head from where he'd been sniffing some remains and coolly eyed the feline shifter. Nemain smiled, baring her teeth at both of them as Jinx leapt up onto her shoulder.

Sigrun rolled her eyes. "Stop baiting them."

Someone used magic to hide the evidence of whatever was here. Viggo's eyes clouded over briefly as he surveyed the area. *The only magic I can see is what was used to cover up what was here. Even the devourer magic has been wiped away.*

"What type of magic remains?" Sigrun asked tightly.

Vanir magic. Viggo's eyes faded back to their normal color. *Someone from Vanaheim has found us.*

Chapter Eight

My mouth watered as the scent of spiced meat drifted over me. Nemain had hunted down one of those deer-like creatures, and Sigrun wasted no time in carving it up and getting it cooking over the fire. Gunnar, Viggo, and the grimalkins helped themselves to what was left.

We'd all agreed going into the caves should wait until the following morning. It had been late afternoon when we came across the meindyr, and none of us wanted to explore the cave system at night. It would be dark no matter what, but some predators actively hunted at night, and it seemed wise to avoid those if we could.

I watched with amusement as Sigrun handed two sticks with meat on them to Isabeau and Finn. The vampire girl immediately tore into hers, only to spit it out because it was too hot. Finn delicately blew on his to cool it down before handing it over to Isabeau and taking hers. Despite their differences, their friendship was deepening. Or maybe it was because they were so different. I was just glad he had a friend who was close to his age, and someone he didn't have to keep his secrets from. Even if he wanted to, Isabeau would be able to detect all of them. I shifted with unease at the implications of Isabeau's growing power. Not out of fear of what she would do but of the fear others would have of her once they knew what she was capable of. She could pluck their secrets out of their minds with such ease. Her life had the potential to be very lonely.

"What are you thinking?" Elisa asked as she plopped down next to me and handed me some food. "You looked sad all of a sudden."

I nibbled on the meat, groaning slightly as the delicious juices dripped down my throat. "Just thinking about future problems. But we have enough to worry about now without borrowing more trouble."

Elisa snorted. "Agreed."

"So when are we going to tell them they're not coming with us tomorrow?" I licked my fingers clean, waiting for Elisa to answer. When no response came, I glanced up and saw she was fixated on my fingers. Realization about what I'd been doing and where her thoughts had gone hit me, and a blush crept up my face. "Elisa?" Her name came out far huskier than I had intended.

"What?" She blinked slowly. Clearly she hadn't heard a word I'd said.

"When are we breaking the news to the kids?" I repeated.

She groaned and tilted her head back. "Not until tomorrow morning. Isabeau won't sleep otherwise."

I nodded and took another bite, chewing slowly as I thought about how that conversation would go. Finn was the complete opposite of Isabeau. She wore her heart on her sleeve while Finn kept everything coiled tightly within him. I didn't know how much of that was the type of person he was or where he'd grown up. Luna and another sidhe had raised Finn, and they'd done their best to protect him. But he'd grown up in a realm full of devourers, among the army of his father, the exiled fae king, Balor.

Neither his father nor his mother had shown Finn an ounce of love. They had viewed him as a means to an end from the start and rarely interacted with him until the past year. At which point, they started monitoring his power growth carefully because they were planning on sacrificing him so Balor could become more powerful. My mother might have abandoned me in a fae realm, but she'd likely done it to protect me. It pissed me off, but that was nothing compared to what Finn's parents had done to him. But he never talked about it and never showed the slightest hint of anger towards them.

"Worried about Finn?" Elisa asked. My gaze slid to hers, and I arched an eyebrow at her. She snickered. "You're not hard to read, at least not to me."

"He won't be happy about being separated tomorrow, but he'll do it. I just wish I knew more about what he was thinking and feeling. He rolls with all these changes so easily, and I kind of wish he wouldn't? I don't know." I paused. "I can protect him from the dangers I understand, and I know all of you can, too. But how do we help him heal from whatever fucked up emotional trauma he has experienced if he won't talk to us about it?"

"I don't know," Elisa said. "The guys and I have had the same conversation about Isabeau. I know it seems like she hides nothing about how she's feeling, but that's not true at all. It's more like she throws all her emotions out in front of her like a shield while holding part of herself back. The look on her face yesterday when she did . . . whatever she did to Viggo. I've never seen that side of her before. She's still months away from her seventh birthday, but that look was so cold."

"We'll figure it out," I said. "In the meantime, I'm glad Isabeau and Finn have each other."

"Me, too."

We finished eating our meal and chatted about lighter

topics. It was nice. Talking with Elisa felt effortless, even if she distracted me every time she ran her tongue over her fangs.

"Have you been with someone?" The thought escaped my lips before I could squash it.

"Been with someone?" She arched a perfectly sculpted eyebrow at me, and I blushed from my head to my toes.

"Dated someone," I pushed out. "With how restricted your life was before you escaped the Council . . . it occurred to me that you may not have had that chance before, and I was just wondering—" I covered my face with a hand. "Feel free to put me out of my misery any time now."

Elisa grinned and patted my knee. "But you're so adorable when you blush." She laughed at whatever she saw on my face but answered my question. "I was nineteen when we got out and tracked down Nemain. We weren't completely isolated where we lived growing up. Several other groups like ours were in the facility, and we had opportunities to interact. We knew the Council guards were keeping an eye on us, but they allowed us some leeway as we got older. If they felt a relationship was becoming too strong, they would break apart the couple, so it was an unspoken rule to keep things to casual flings or at least make sure it appeared that way."

"And did you?" I bit my lip. "Have casual flings?"

"Yes." Elisa eyed me. "Does that bother you?"

"No, not at all." I rushed the words out. "Honestly it would have freaked me out if you hadn't ever. . ." I trailed off before I blushed like an idiot again.

"Done the horizontal tango? Taken a roll in the hay? Knocked boots?"

"You delight in tormenting me, don't you?"

"Absolutely." She grinned at me. "What about you?"

"I dated a few sidhe girls over the years. Nothing ever got that serious." When she waggled her eyebrows at me suggestively, I rolled my eyes. "I've knocked boots."

"Hussy." We both dissolved into giggles.

Sigrun and Nemain stood up from the campfire and headed over to us, leaving Damon and Misha to deal with Isabeau. Finn was already curled up and asleep with the two grimalkins wrapped around him.

"I'm going to check in with Magos and Mikhail to make sure they're ready tomorrow morning," Nemain said. "I'll be back soon." She headed farther into the woods.

Sigrun took a seat across from us. "Ask me whatever questions you have, and I'll do my best to answer them. I'll spend some time with Magos in the morning to discuss a training strategy for you."

Annoyance flickered through me at the reminder of my time with her being limited and I started to argue, but Elisa grabbed my hand and squeezed it. I clicked my mouth shut and gave Sigrun a cool look when her gaze flickered towards our clasped hands and smiled slightly.

"What type of magic do valkyries possess?" Elisa asked. "Some of it, at least, is telepathic in nature, correct?"

Sigrun tilted her head to the side as she studied Elisa. "This is a conversation for me and Bryn. You should run along and join the others, *vampire*."

I bristled, but Elisa squeezed my hand tighter. "I will do no such thing. And please keep in mind that while you might be able to best me in a physical fight, when it comes to verbal sparring, I will run circles around you. I grew up amongst the Council, I thrived in their political bullshit, and I spend a substantial amount of my free time with Pele, whereas you spend your days with a silent wolf and taciturn cat. Insult me all you like, *valkyrie*, but you will answer my questions."

"Will I?"

My muscles tightened at the challenge in those two words, getting ready to surge between them if I had to, but Elisa never let go of my hand.

"Yes." Elisa leaned back and smiled coldly at the valkyrie. "Bryn is frustrated and disappointed in you for failing to help her when she needs it most. But that's nothing compared to the guilt and disappointment you're feeling against yourself for failing to step the fuck up."

A muscle in Sigrun's jaw ticked.

"I know seeing another valkyrie brings up all sorts of emotional baggage for you and you would prefer to waste your knowledge and skills for the rest of your life while you hide away in this realm. But you are not unique. Everyone in this clearing has suffered and shredded parts of their soul to survive and help those they love survive. So you will answer my questions because it's the least you can do to assuage the guilt you're feeling, and because Bryn very much wants to bury her shiny new axe into your side for the way you're speaking to me. Until both of you cool your heads, I will ask the questions that need to be asked and you will answer them. We clear, *valkyrie?*"

I gawked at Elisa. Part of me was horrified that I'd allowed her to fight my battles with Sigrun. But another part of me was so incredibly turned on that I wanted to grab the vampire and find some dark corner of the forest to show her exactly how damn much I liked her.

While I struggled to get my hormones under control, Sigrun stared at Elisa, that faint red glow stirring briefly in her eyes. After a few tense seconds she smiled faintly. "Crystal."

"When Bryn first awakened, we were being attacked by some fae with devourer magic. I'm assuming Nemain filled you in on that?" Sigrun nodded. "Bryn was able to unleash some sort of psychic attack on the fae. Jinx and Finn threw up a shield around us, so we only got a small taste. But the fae who were hit directly by it died. It cut through all their defenses. What was that? And how does she do it again?"

"Geðveiki." Sigrun grimaced. "As you already noted, much

of our magic is telepathic in nature. We can cast minor illusion spells, for example."

Elisa jerked, and I glanced back and forth between her and Sigrun. Elisa blinked a few times as she stared at the valkyrie, but I didn't see anything different. "What?" I asked. "What do you see?"

"Her wings are gone," Elisa whispered. "And she seems . . . less. I don't know how to describe it. She still looks like herself, but what makes her so utterly terrifying is gone."

"Glad to know you have the common sense to be scared of me, despite your speech earlier." That small smile briefly appeared again. "My wings are still there and nothing about me has changed. I simply made it so your mind no longer perceived them."

Elisa frowned. "What if I touched them?"

"That takes a little more work on my part, but I could still make it so your mind didn't recognize the touch. The more senses I need to trick, the harder it is to pull off. It doesn't work on other valkyries or most of the species that dwell in the realms of Yggdrasil. Viggo can do the same, but his magic is stronger than mine in this regard. He can hide from almost every species with little effort."

"What is geðveiki?" My tongue stumbled over the pronunciation. The invisibility trick would be useful to learn, but I was more interested in whatever the hell I had done to the fae soldiers.

"It's a direct telepathic attack that causes intense blinding pain. If the attack goes on for longer than a few seconds, it leads to hemorrhaging and death."

I thought about how the fae warriors had clenched their heads before blood poured out of their eyes, noses, and mouths. Some small part of me wondered if I should feel guilty over not only causing their deaths but making it so painful. My gaze drifted over to where Finn slept, and whatever small part of me thought about that vanished. They knew who they served, and they did it willingly. I wouldn't feel regret at harming anyone who came after Finn.

"How do I do it again? And can I control it?" It wouldn't be much of a weapon if it harmed my friends along with my enemies. I was fairly confident it would never target Finn, but less so of anyone else. I remembered almost nothing from the immediate events after I'd died and been reborn as a valkyrie. Just the red haze of rage.

Sigrun shook her head. "I would suggest you don't do it again. Geðveiki is a weapon of war, and it can only be directed, not fully controlled. It doesn't work against other valkyries and there are some ways to defend against it, but those are known only by the Aesir and Vanir. It cannot be wielded often, and because of that, plus its chaotic nature, there is no way to practice with it."

"It worked exceptionally well against the fae," I argued. "I can't ignore such a weapon. You told me to make use of my resources earlier. Is this not a resource?"

"It will never be one you can fully control. I'm not saying there won't come a time when you will wield it again, but you can't practice with it nor fully plan how to use it. You're young and it will take some time to fully come into your magic. The bond impacts your magic, and I have no idea how being bonded to not only a fae, but *that* fae, is going to affect you. It will probably be at least a year before you could unleash geðveiki the way you did upon your awakening. The longer you wait before yielding it again, the stronger the impact will be."

I thought of the rage I had felt earlier when Gunnar attacked Elisa. "I thought I felt it start to rise earlier. How do I stop it if that's the case?"

"That wasn't the geðveiki, it was just bloodlust." Sigrun shrugged and tossed another log into the fire. "The bloodlust rises first, and then, if you have enough magic built up, you can also unleash the geðveiki."

"So if she doesn't want to use geðveiki in the future," Elisa cut in, "she needs to give into the bloodlust."

Sigrun nodded. "Sometimes there is no stopping it. But most of the time, you can channel that fury in other ways, and that will be enough. In the past, the valkyries would try hard to not use geðveiki, partly because it was so chaotic in nature, but mostly because it takes time for it to recharge and you never know when you might truly need it."

"All right, no driving our enemies insane and making their minds explode unless absolutely necessary," Elisa said calmly, as if anything in that sentence was normal. I stared at her, and she grinned. "Look, in terms of freaky powers, Nemain still has all of us beat."

"She's not wrong," Nemain said from where she thunked down next to me. I jumped several inches before twisting to scowl at her. She just grinned unrepentantly. "We'll have to work on you minding your surroundings."

I turned to Elisa. "Did you see her coming?" She shook her head slowly as she stared at Nemain, wide-eyed. "Where did you come from?" I narrowed my eyes at Nemain. Elisa would have seen her if she'd been creeping up behind me.

"The trees," Sigrun said, amusement lighting up her eyes. "You're a valkyrie, Bryn. You, more than anyone, should know that death often comes from above."

Chapter Nine

"No!" Isabeau yelled from where she was perched at the top of a tree. She had been less than pleased about being informed she would not be joining us on the cave adventure. We'd all anticipated her being angry about being sent home; what we had not anticipated was her leaping ten feet straight up onto a branch and quickly climbing to the top of a tree. Elisa had been trying to talk her down for the past five minutes after Misha had teleported up to where Isabeau was sitting and attempted to grab her. He was sporting a split lip and a black eye although it was rapidly healing.

"Will you be okay at the apartment without me?" I asked Finn.

"Yes."

I waited to see if he had anything else to add, but he remained silent. I bit back my sigh. He was likely almost as upset as Isabeau at being sent back, but unlike her, Finn kept his feelings hidden. "Luna is going to go back with you," I said.

"Jinx isn't happy," he said quietly.

"No." I laughed. "Honestly, I'm surprised he's not up there in the tree with Isabeau throwing a tantrum."

A small tentative grin tugged at Finn's lips, and I celebrated inwardly, then cursed as a large pinecone thumped onto my head. I rubbed the sore spot and glanced up in time to see another one fall off the branch. I stepped to the side and narrowly avoided another hit to the head.

Careful, valkyrie. Jinx's voice grumbled in my head. *Bad luck would be a terrible thing to have while wandering around in a dark cave.*

The black grimalkin stalked off, and I stared after him. I hadn't even known he'd been there. "Did you know he was behind us?" Finn's grin blossomed into a smile, and I snorted while I ruffled his hair. "You're definitely picking up some bad habits from these miscreants."

"This is ridiculous!" Nemain snapped and stretched out her hand. The air to her right rippled slightly, and a gateway snapped into existence, revealing Magos and Mikhail waiting in the apartment. They both stepped through and lifted their gaze to where Isabeau sat. Magos raised his eyebrows while Mikhail just laughed quietly. "One of you is getting her down!" Nemain growled.

Magos smiled. "I think a solution will present itself momentarily."

As if on cue, the front door to the apartment opened and Kaysea breezed in. The beautiful and sinfully curvy mermaid glided across the floor and joined us on the other side of the gateway. She didn't even glance in Isabeau's direction, but instead went straight to Finn and held out a plate full of cookies and cupcakes. "Zareen baked these this morning. Would you like one?"

Finn stared at the plate as he carefully debated which one to try.

Nemain snatched a cookie covered in some type of blue frosting off the plate and grinned as Kaysea scowled at her. "So did you just happen to swing by Zareen's house this

84

morning to pick these up? Or were you already there?" Nemain asked slyly.

Kaysea narrowed her eyes at Nemain as she swept some of her green hair back behind her ear. "We were having breakfast."

"After having dinner last night?" Nemain arched an eyebrow.

"Are those cupcakes?" Isabeau interrupted. "What type of frosting?"

"Bless you, Kaysea," Elisa murmured.

"These are red velvet with cream cheese frosting. I have more in the downstairs apartment."

Isabeau pondered this information. "How many more? And are they different flavors?"

"You'll have to come with me to find out." Kaysea smirked. While Isabeau pondered this information, I snagged one of the sugary treats for myself. The sweet flavors exploded across my tongue, and I closed my eyes as I savored it.

The snap of a branch had me opening my eyes and glancing up just in time to see Isabeau dropping through the air and landing on another branch ten feet beneath her. She stepped off that one, causing my heart to stutter as she landing on a much thinner branch, repeating the move until she landed on the ground.

"Please don't ever do that," I told Finn. "I don't think my heart could take it."

Finn didn't so much as glance at me, all of his attention was focused on the plate of treats. Slowly, he reached out and took one of the cookies in the shape of a seashell.

"You can have as many as you want, Finn," Kaysea said gently. "Zareen is going to come by later, and we're going to make cannolis."

"What are cannolis?" Isabeau asked as she grabbed a cookie with one hand and a cupcake with the other.

"They're delicious." Kaysea smiled as the young vampire girl shoved the whole cookie into her mouth. "It's fried dough with a sweet filling. You'll love them."

"Okay," Isabeau said around a mouthful of cookie. She glanced at her vampire siblings. "I'm still mad at all of you." Grabbing another cookie off the plate, she skipped through the gateway and back into the apartment.

"Are you ready, Finn?" Kaysea asked. He nodded and gave me a little wave, then followed after Isabeau. Luna leapt down from where she'd been observing all this unfold and joined Finn and Isabeau in the apartment. Kaysea held the plate out to Misha and Damon, and they fell on the remaining treats as if they were starving wolves discovering a deer carcass. Elisa rolled her eyes. "Connor is already at the apartment on the second floor. He'll probably stay out of sight because I doubt he has the patience for the kids, but he'll be there if we need him."

Nemain's lips tugged downward in distaste, but she nodded.

"Who is Connor?" I asked. The name sounded familiar, but I couldn't place it.

"My brother," Kaysea said. "He's . . . umm . . . an acquired taste."

"He's an ass," Nemain and Sigrun said at the same time.

"Connor isn't a people person," Kaysea countered. "But he is a good fighter. He has served as guardian to the Tír fo Thuinn throne for centuries." Neither Nemain nor Sigrun argued with her statement.

I found it amusing that Kaysea was apparently the opposite of her brother in both personality and skills. Kaysea could defend herself with water magic, lethally if she wanted to, but she wasn't a warrior. And her kindness was genuine. I would have liked her for the kindness she showed to Finn alone, but she had also played an intricate role in bringing all of us together, and thus saving Finn's life. I would forever be in her debt, despite her claiming no debt existed between us.

"We'll probably be difficult to contact for the next day or so," Nemain said. "But you know how to contact my brother?"

"Yes. Cian would probably enjoy baking with us all afternoon." Kaysea paused and tapped a finger against her lips. "Although I'm not sure I could deal with both Dante and Connor in the same room."

"I think I might actually pay to see that," Sigrun replied.

Elisa saw my confused expression. "Dante is Cian's partner," she explained. "He can be a bit grumpy sometimes."

"Lover," Nemain corrected. "I'm sure Cian will come to his senses any day now and dump his ass."

"Haven't they been together for almost two centuries?" Elisa quirked an eyebrow at Nemain.

"And didn't *you* try to pick Dante up before he met your brother?" Mikhail asked, his features arranged in angelic innocence.

"Nobody asked you, vampire!" Nemain snapped.

Mikhail grinned at her, and Magos casually moved to stand between them. I gave Elisa a bewildered look, and she mouthed, *I'll tell you later*.

"Well," Kaysea drew out. "Have fun!" She took the empty plate with her back through the gateway and waved at all of us as Nemain closed it.

"Now what?" Misha asked, wiping the back of his hand against his mouth. I couldn't help but be a little impressed at how quickly he and Damon had eaten the remaining cupcakes and cookies. Food really did just disappear around the two of them.

Sigrun glanced up at the early morning sky and then at me. "We'll practice for an hour and then venture into the cave."

She turned towards Magos. "I'm assuming you're familiar with fighting with a shield and axe?"

"Yes."

"I will show Bryn some basic moves, and then you and I will spar to demonstrate those moves. We'll do this again later tonight and tomorrow morning so she has some basics down and can continue to practice with you. I will teach her other lessons regarding valkyrie magic throughout the day."

Magos frowned. "Will you not be able to continue teaching her? I thought Nemain wanted you to be Bryn's mentor? There is much you can teach her, and you'll need more than a few days to do that."

"No shit," I muttered.

"I will teach her what I can and then all of you will leave," Sigrun said.

Magos studied her with his striking copper eyes and gave her a shallow nod. "If that is all you can give, then we are grateful for your time."

Sigrun flinched at his words but recovered quickly and strode over to a small clearing, beckoning me to follow her. She put me through the paces of several simple moves, correcting my footing and body position for each one. My movements were slow at first, but after a few rounds, Sigrun was satisfied with my progress.

"You should continue to practice with a sword in addition to the shield and axe," Sigrun said. "Also, work a spear into the routine."

"Why?" I asked. "If a shield and axe will be my primary weapons, shouldn't I only practice with them?"

"Because you need to understand how the other weapons work to properly fight against them," Magos answered.

"Exactly," Sigrun said. "Magos and I will spar, and I'm going to only use the moves I demonstrated to you."

Sigrun tucked her wings in tight as she took up a fighting

stance. I handed my shield to Magos, and he attached it to his arm. He moved it around a few times, with fluid, natural movements that made me a little jealous. It still felt so clunky to me.

"This is gonna be amazing," Misha said as he stared at the two warriors with awe. Despite my frustration towards Sigrun, I had to agree with him. Sigrun and Magos were two sides of the same coin. Mikhail and Nemain were both tall with muscular builds, but they were dwarfed by Magos. He matched Sigrun's height and, like her, he was broad with slabs of muscle. Unlike Sigrun, Magos dressed to play down his warrior nature. He favored daemon attire more similar to suits than the fighting leathers Sigrun wore. There was no hiding his warrior physique, but Magos carried himself with an elegant civility Sigrun lacked.

Magos held his hand out to the side, and mist coiled around it, solidifying in a sword that looked plain compared to the ones I'd seen the fae wield over the realms. No fancy etchings adorned the steel, nor were there any jewels or stones embedded in the hilt. Sigrun took in the sword, and genuine admiration lit up her face.

I knew exactly how she felt. Something about that sword demanded respect. I was a little confused about why Mikhail didn't have a similar sword. From what I understood, Magos's ability to call the sword was related to the species that Magos and Mikhail originally were before they became vampires. I'd tried to ask Nemain about it, but it was one of the few times she had shut me down.

Sigrun was still smiling when she shoved her shield forward, forcing Magos to dodge, and quickly followed up with an axe strike. I sucked in a breath as the vampire warrior twisted to the side, letting the axe slide by, and then spun quickly. He struck at Sigrun's exposed side, and she narrowly managed to shift her shield in time to block it. They bared their teeth at each other in happy grins and broke apart. It had all happened so fast, I barely had time to process their moves. They clashed over and over again.

Gradually, I started to see the pattern in Sigrun's movements. She was using the same three moves just like she told me she would, but even with the limited number of movements, she could chain them together in different ways. I'd been thinking of the shield in terms of defense only, but it was clear from watching Sigrun that I had been wrong about that. She used the shield to muscle Magos around and bashed it into his side several times. If he'd been a weaker opponent, she would have broken bones with those hits.

But using the shield in such a way left her open for attack, and Magos seized on the opening several times. Several of the moves on both their parts were sloppy, and they never would have used them in a real fight. They were both deliberately demonstrating the strengths and weaknesses of each type of attack. Sigrun seemed to be enjoying the hell out of the fight, and I suddenly felt sad at the idea of her living in this realm with nothing but the wolf and skogkatt for company. She and Nemain clearly had a friendship, even if neither was willing to call it that. But did she have anyone else in her life? Anyone else to sit around the campfire with and talk about life? Anyone else to spar with? I'd been so caught up in what I needed from Sigrun, I hadn't thought about what Sigrun might need from us.

Shame ran through me. I'd been so caught up in my own problems that all I'd been was critical of Sigrun since arriving here. My parents had raised me better than this. I needed to convince Sigrun to mentor me, and not just because I needed the help. Steely determination replaced the frustration and anger I'd been feeling towards the old valkyrie. Even if I couldn't change her mind today, I wouldn't give up. I'd find a way to make this work.

The clang of steel against steel pulled me from my

thoughts. Magos had slipped through Sigrun's shield defense, but she'd parried his strike with her axe. They faced each other, both dripping in sweat, before taking a step back and bowing slightly.

"Good match," Magos said.

Sigrun nodded. I didn't miss the sorrow that briefly flickering across her face. She'd enjoyed that, and it confirmed my suspicions that Sigrun was lonely even if she wouldn't admit it. When Sigrun looked at me, I made sure to wipe any emotions from my face. Something told me that she wouldn't react well to pity.

"You could be a strong fighter just by mastering those three moves alone, but I will teach you a few more tonight," she said. "I know it is tempting to learn as many moves as possible, but you will be more successful by mastering a few of them and, more importantly, knowing when to use which move and how to chain them together. That will come with experience."

"Thank you for the lesson," I said. "It was helpful to see those moves in action and how well they can be used in a fight."

Sigrun narrowed her eyes at me. Clearly this wasn't the response she expected. I did my best to impersonate the calm, neutral smile Elisa so often used when she was trying to sway a conversation in a certain direction. The valkyrie narrowed her eyes further. *Note to self, work on innocent smile.*

"You're getting slow, my feathered friend," Nemain said as she swaggered up to us.

Sigrun flipped the axe in her hand a few times. "You think so?"

Nemain gestured at the numerous places Magos had scored hits on the valkyrie's body. "You've gotten lazy while enjoying your retirement. When's the last time you fought against a worthy opponent before we came to visit?"

"Is that what this is? A visit?" Sigrun said evenly. Something told me they'd had this exact conversation many times before. "I thought this was you not respecting my boundaries yet again."

"Your boundaries are boring."

"Not all of us see the line in the sand and decide to set it on fire, mongrel."

Nemain grinned, displaying her fangs. "Mongrel is really more of an insult directed at canines. Despite the fae and . . . otherness . . . in me, my feline nature reigns supreme."

"More's the pity," Sigrun complained.

Nemain pulled her twin blades free. Unlike Magos's plain sword, Nemain's blades were pretty. Which made sense because they were fae made, and the fae couldn't help but make things pretty, sometimes in impractical ways. Intricate knots were inlaid in the silver blades, and several dark blue gems were embedded in the hilts. Despite the beautiful appearance of the blades, they were strong, and Nemain wielded them with ruthless efficiency.

Excitement surged through me. While the vampire boys had been excited to see Magos and Sigrun spar, I was more interested in this. Nemain brought an intensity to everything she did that I couldn't help but be drawn into this.

"We should get going," Sigrun said, even as she eyed Nemain's blades with interest. "All the nocturnal beasties should have returned to their lairs and daylight hides for now."

"The caves are going to be dull, and I need to burn off some energy." Nemain tilted her head to the side in a way that reminded me of Jinx studying something he wanted to eat. "Unless that little fight with Magos tired out the mighty valkyrie?"

Sigrun let out a long sigh and, faster than I could track, swung her axe directly at Nemain's head. I leapt back and was vaguely aware of the others doing the same. Nemain slid out of the path of Sigrun's axe on liquid joints and struck at the valkyrie's side. Sigrun's shield snapped into existence and blocked the strike. Nemain danced back, laughter pouring from her.

We watched as the two danced around the clearing. This fight was so much different from the one Sigrun had just had with Magos. The two of them had similar fighting styles that relied more on brute strength. Their fight had been them beating on each other, trying to break through the other's defense based on strength and skill. Nemain was no match for Sigrun when it came to strength.

But holy gods, she was fast.

Sigrun swung her axe in a powerful strike aimed at Nemain's abdomen. I sucked in a breath at the same time as Damon and Misha. But the feline shifter leapt over the strike, body spinning in midair, and cut several of Sigrun's braids off. She snatched them out of the air and cackled as she tossed them back at the valkyrie. "You *are* getting slow," she taunted.

The valkyrie bellowed, and her wings snapped open. She leapt into the sky and dove at Nemain, who only laughed in delight as she dodged the attack.

"I think Nemain might be insane," I said as we watched her dodge another axe strike, only for Sigrun to bash her shield into the shifter. Nemain went flying across the clearing but flipped midair to land on her feet. She flicked her head back and gave Sigrun a bloody grin before running back towards her.

"Because she thinks trading blows with a pissed off valkyrie is a good time?" Elisa asked, amusement clear in her voice. "If she's insane, what does that make him?" I followed her gaze to where Mikhail was leaning against a tree on the other side of the clearing. He was watching Nemain with those intense dark twilight eyes of his. His expression definitely held lust, but something else too, something that took me a moment to place.

Longing.

His gaze snapped to mine as he noticed our attention on him. His features returned to the usual arrogant, flat expression he normally wore, and I quickly looked away.

"They're so confusing," I whispered to Elisa.

She laughed softly. "I think they're more confusing to each other."

Chapter Ten

"So on a scale of one to ten, how dark exactly is it going to be?" Misha asked from where we all peered into the cave.

"You're a vampire," Nemain said. "You can see in absolute darkness."

"Yeah, but it's the principle of the thing."

I snorted. When I was younger, I'd explored several cave systems in the mountains with some of the local fae kids. Sometimes cracks in the ceiling would allow light from the surface to filter in, but more often than not, the caves got dark quickly and stayed that way. I wasn't afraid of the dark, but it wasn't exactly my favorite thing. Add the often tight spaces found in caves, and I was really not looking forward to this. As much as I missed Finn, I was glad he was safe in the apartment.

"Last time I was in these caves, there was no source of light. It will be pitch black within minutes of us entering," Sigrun said as she pulled several light orange marbles from a pouch on her belt. She tossed them into the air, and they hung there for a moment before glowing faintly. "One of the vampires should take the lead and another should guard our backs." Gunnar let out a low woof, causing the corners of Sigrun's lips to tilt up. "Gunnar will walk with the vampire who leads us. He won't be able to see all that well, but his sense of smell is the best out of everyone here."

"Can you understand him?" I asked curiously as my gaze flickered between them. Viggo was clearly telepathic, but Gunnar hadn't communicated with me or any of the others as far as I could tell.

Sigrun shrugged. "Well enough. He doesn't speak if that's what you're asking, but that doesn't mean he's not intelligent."

Debatable, Viggo said. The white wolf swung his head towards the skogkatt and licked his lips.

"Don't start, you two," Sigrun warned.

"I'll take the lead," Mikhail volunteered. "The kids should be in the middle."

I bristled at being referred to as a kid, but I was beginning to accept I would just have to get used to that. Maybe when I celebrated my two hundredth birthday they'd upgrade me to young adult.

"Jinx, stay with Magos, and keep your senses open for any magic," Nemain said. The bruise that had covered the left side of her face was still faintly visible. Sigrun had gotten in some good hits, but Nemain didn't seem bothered by it in the least.

Fine. But I'm not touching the floor. It's probably sticky.

"Why would it be sticky?" Nemain asked.

The last cave we were in was sticky and covered in bat shit.

"That was in a completely different realm," Nemain said. "We don't even know if there are bats here."

"It's fine," Magos cut in and extended his left arm. Jinx trotted over to the vampire, changing in a blink to his smaller glamoured form. He leapt onto Magos's arm and climbed up to perch on his shoulder, claws digging into clothes and probably flesh for balance. I couldn't help my wince, but Magos didn't so much as flinch.

"We should be as quiet as possible while we're in there," Sigrun said.

"Damon, think you can link us up telepathically?" Nemain asked.

I shifted uncomfortably. We'd tried this before, and while Damon's magic was able to link my mind to the others, I knew it was hard for him.

"Maybe leave me out and someone can tap my shoulder or something if you need to communicate with me?" I offered.

"Why?" Sigrun looked at me with raised eyebrows.

"It's hard for the others to communicate with me telepathically," I said, trying and failing to keep the frustration out of my voice. "We've tried practicing, but it doesn't seem to help. Everything comes through muffled or not at all."

"How long has it been since you used the geðveiki?"

"About three months."

Sigrun nodded. "Unleashing the geðveiki takes a lot out of you, and sometimes your mind will put up guards afterward to protect itself. You will need to lower them."

"How?" I frowned. "I don't feel anything."

"Close your eyes," she ordered. Feeling a little silly, I did as she asked. "Concentrate only on the sound of my voice."

I can feel the guards you have placed around your mind. Sigrun's voice came through faint, as if she was standing far away. *Continue to concentrate on my voice but think of it as a string that connects me to you. Follow that string.*

Sigrun repeated the words over and over, and I focused on them. It felt strange at first, but then it started to click. I followed after the words, only to hit a wall.

That is the defensive wall your mind crafted to protect you from mental attacks. It's impressively strong for one so young. You need to practice lowering it and raising it. Just like any weapon, it will eventually become instinctual, but for now, you will need to practice.

How? I pushed the word out, unsure if Sigrun would hear it or not.

Everyone has a different way of doing things. After all, this is all in your mind. I felt the sugary taste of amusement behind her words. *Try envisioning it as a gate you are raising or lowering. You can change it as you see fit.*

I thought of the large silver and gold gate that guarded the city at the base of the mountains where I'd grown up. I envisioned the thick chains that controlled the gate and pulled them down. The fog that had stood between me and Sigrun evaporated.

Good job. Now lower them.

I did as she requested, and we went through the process a couple more times until I was comfortable with it. It still felt clunky and took me a few seconds to make the change, but I reminded myself that I used to feel awkward wielding a sword, and now it was almost second nature to me. The ease of doing this would come with time.

"I'm ready." I nodded to Damon.

Can you hear me?

Loud and clear. I smiled broadly at him.

Let's go, Sigrun said, moving to stand next to Mikhail. One of the orange marbles trailed after her while the others spread out above us. Gunnar and Viggo fell into step behind them, the latter making a strike at the wolf when it got too close. Elisa and I walked side-by-side with the others behind us. I'd wrapped my wings around myself like a cloak, but with each step, the air got colder, and I could already feel it seep into my bones. If Elisa was bothered by this, she didn't show it.

Are you not cold? I asked.

Elisa slid me a glance. *The cold doesn't really bother vampires. I don't know why.*

It's because the devourer species used to create vampires came from a frozen wasteland of a realm, Nemain said. Even telepathically, I could tell she was only partly paying attention to this conversation; the rest of her was focused on the cave and our surroundings.

You've seen them? Elisa perked up. *What are they called?*

They don't have a name. If there was a species capable of speaking in that realm, they died off long ago. I still remember the feeling of that icy wind on my face. It hurt. Jinx and I noped on out of there in less than an hour.

Why were you there to begin with? Mikhail asked.

Nemain didn't answer right away, and I didn't know if that was because she didn't want to answer the question or because she specifically did not want to answer Mikhail. *It was after my parents died and before I met Sebastian. My magic had always been difficult to control when I was a child, but I came fully into my power after . . . after everything happened.*

Thoughts of what had happened to Nemain's parents started to pop into my mind, but I shoved them down hard so that Nemain wouldn't pick up on any of them. Kaysea had told me the story after I had picked up pieces of it and asked the mermaid to clarify some things. It was obvious it still caused Nemain pain to speak of it. Watching your parents die while you could do nothing would do that to a person.

I was too unstable, Nemain continued. *Terrified I would hurt my brother, so I left. Jinx and I traveled around, at first only to uninhabited realms, but later on we went to many of the daemon and fae realms.*

Was that when you met Pele and Kaysea? Elisa asked.

Yes. I met Pele first. She was my light in the dark for a long time. Then I had an unfortunate incident in one of the fae realms, and Kaysea intervened on my behalf.

That's a nice way of saying she saved your ass, Jinx said.

We were only in trouble because we were helping her, Nemain bristled. *Besides, you were there too, and it's not like you were all that helpful.*

Jinx sniffed but didn't say anything. Damon and Misha peppered Nemain with questions about all the realms she had visited, but I mostly tuned them out. We were now completely dependent on the light given off by the glowing orbs that floated above us, and I had to concentrate on where I was stepping. The vampires could still see everything, and when I glanced over my shoulder at Nemain, her pupils were almost completely dilated. She would be able to see well enough. The passage narrowed, and I tried to ignore the unsettling feeling of the walls closing in. Elisa pressed into my side, the back of her hand brushing mine. The sensation was enough for me to tamp down the claustrophobic thoughts. I hadn't had my wings for long, but I already found the idea of being trapped somewhere I couldn't fly disturbing.

If I remember correctly, the passage will stay narrow like this for another mile before opening up again. At that point it will split off into a few different directions, and we'll have to figure out where to go, Sigrun said.

Elisa, why don't you shift to a wolf and see if you can pick up any scents? Maybe you or Gunnar will detect something that will help us determine which path to take, Nemain suggested.

Sure. The coarse fur of Elisa's coat brushed my hand a second later. My fingers dug into her coat, and she leaned into my touch before joining Gunnar, where he walked a few paces in front of Mikhail and Sigrun. Without her calming presence, some of the tension returned to my body, and I fought the urge to unwrap my wings and flex them. I needed a distraction; otherwise, I would lose it after another ten minutes of this.

Sigrun, yesterday while fighting, I somehow shot feathers out of my wings as if they were spears. I don't really know how I did it though or how often I can do it.

Spjót feathers. Sigrun looked over her shoulder at me and grinned. *They're thin feathers tucked into our primary feathers. They have no impact on our ability to fly, but when we perform certain movements, they will shoot out and impale our enemies. It will take a few days, but new ones will grow.*

Oh. I thought about how I had spun in a tight circle when they'd been released. *Would you show me what type of maneuvers will trigger their release when we're out of this cave?*

Yes.

Even in the dim lighting, I could see Sigrun's wings wrap rigidly around her as she waited for me to push her about more training. Instead, I asked her about her life here, in this realm. About what she, Viggo, and Gunnar did most days. At first she kept her answers short, but gradually, with Damon and Misha's help, her answers became longer. Even Magos and Mikhail chimed in to ask her questions.

What do you do with Viggo if you and Gunnar fly somewhere? I asked, frowning at where the skogkatt kept pace beside the valkyrie. *Do you carry him?*

Sigrun scoffed, and Gunnar let out a chuffing noise that sounded suspiciously like laughter. I started to ask another question, or apologize, I wasn't really sure what I planning, when Viggo whirled and leapt into the air. And stayed there. I didn't even realize I'd stopped walking until Damon bumped into me, his mouth gaping open as we both stared at the shaggy brown skogkatt as he moved through the air as if jumping from one invisible lily pad to another.

Just because I don't need something as pedestrian as wings doesn't mean I'm not capable of traveling through the air, Viggo growled as he ran circles around me and the vampire boys. The passage was too small for me to turn and keep track of him, so I had to keep twisting my head to watch him, which made me feel a little dizzy. Just as he entered my blind spot, I felt him land on my shoulder, and I stumbled slightly from the impact. He shoved off and returned to Sigrun's side, giving me one last dirty look.

How long can you travel like that? I asked, still more than a little bewildered at seeing the cat walk on air.

Longer than you can fly, he boasted.

He can't stop when he's in the air, Jinx said snidely. *If he stops moving, he drops like a stone.*

You'll drop like a stone when I throw you off a cliff, grimalkin.

A low growl rumbled from Jinx, and I was suddenly rather nervous about being between the two of them. I really didn't want to end this day covered in scratches from getting in the middle of a literal cat fight. Nemain murmured something quietly to Jinx, and his growl faded to a raspy laugh that rumbled through my head. Feline brawl avoided. I turned the conversation to lighter topics as we continued our way through the cave.

Suddenly, all the vampires stopped moving and the rest of us stopped with them. Elisa's wolf ears perked up, and I strained to hear whatever they were listening to, but all I heard was silence. I waited, willing myself to stay still and not distract them.

Finally, Misha spoke. *There is something ahead. A lot of some-things actually.*

A lot as in more than twenty? Nemain asked. *More than fifty?*

It's hard to tell, Damon said. *They're not moving all that much, more like shuffling their feet occasionally. And . . . they're not breathing.*

Nemain grumbled something, and Sigrun's shoulders tightened. *It could be anything,* Sigrun said.

It's the gods damn draugr and you know it! Nemain snapped.

Let's keep moving, Sigrun said, and pushed past Gunnar and Elisa to take the lead. One glowing orb followed her, and inky blackness stretched in the distance between her and us. Elisa looked back at Nemain, waiting for a command, while Gunnar and Viggo trotted off into the darkness after the valkyrie.

What are the draugr? I asked, staring in the direction Sigrun had gone. Something about them and their potential presence here had set Sigrun off.

Nemain sighed. *You'll see in a few minutes. Come on, let's not let*

Sigrun get too far ahead. She might start the fight without us, and I hate being left out.

Mikhail moved to allow Nemain to take the lead, and we all followed her. Elisa dropped back to walk beside me, and I intertwined my fingers in her coarse fur. An unsettling feeling lodged into my chest with every step, and I knew it was because something was in this cave that shouldn't be there, that shouldn't be in this realm at all.

Chapter Eleven

WHAT THE FUCK IS THAT? Damon asked from the ledge where we all peered down into the wide gap below. The drop to the ground on this side of the cavern was at least twenty feet.

The dim light from the orbs barely managed to penetrate the darkness, and I had to squint to make out the creatures below. I might not be able to see them all that well, but I could definitely smell them. Thanks to years of hunting and butchering my own game, I had a strong stomach. But the sickly sweet smell of decay still coated my throat and nostrils. I was impressed Nemain and the vampires weren't gagging.

My eyes adjusted a little more, and I watched as a dark shape shuffled up the opposite side where the drop-off wasn't as steep.

I grimaced as the thing that used to be a human climbed up the slope, its gait uneven. Others soon joined it as they ambled around the cavern with no clear purpose in mind. Torn and shredded fabric covered their emaciated bodies, pale bluish skin peeking through. A few wore no clothing at all, showing sunken abdomens and protruding ribs. Their faces were the worst part, and I was certain this was what I would be seeing in my nightmares for years to come. The hair had long since fallen from their heads, and between that and their death-tainted skin, their eyes and mouths stood out starkly against their haunted features. Some of them still had noses, but most only had slits instead. They had been human once, or something like it, but now they were empty shells.

Draugr, Jinx spat from where he lay crouched near the edge. His golden eyes tracking the movement below.

Why do I feel this way? I asked, still unable to tear my gaze away from the broken creatures who slowly moved around, completely unaware of our presence. Elisa had shifted back to her vampire form, and she leaned against me. The warmth of her skin on mine helped settle my mind a little, and I used it as a shield against the wrongness.

Because of how they're made, Sigrun said. *It's a dark practice from Vanaheim. The type of magic practiced there is known as seidr. On its own, it's neither good nor bad; that is solely determined by the practitioner.* She looked at me, and I met her deep brown eyes. *The wrongness you're feeling is because we are sensitive to the darker aspects of seidr magic. Valkyries always have been. One of our tasks throughout history has been to hunt down dark practitioners.*

The draugr are created by raising the dead and calling their souls back from Helheim. Souls that are already dark work best. In the process, their souls are twisted and bonded to an item before being shoved back in their bodies. When they rise, they no longer remember who they once were; nothing of them remains. Only the need to be close to the item their soul is bonded with. They do not feel pain or fear. Only hunger.

I tore my gaze away from Sigrun and studied the draugr once more. The need to destroy them and remove them from this world was still a driving force within me, but I couldn't help but feel pity for them. They hadn't asked to become this. *What will happen to their souls when they die?*

They can't die, Nemain said. *They're already dead.*

You know what I mean, I pushed. There was something they weren't telling me.

Neither Nemain nor Sigrun answered. Both wore neutral masks that told me they were hiding something. I turned to face Mikhail and Magos to see if they had any answers, but they merely shook their heads. *I have never come across draugr before.* Mikhail shrugged.

Nor have I, Magos said.

Throughout Helheim, a strong cold wind blows, Viggo said, with none of the snideness I'd come to associate with his voice. *At first, you think the wind is upsetting because it freezes your skin on contact and your very bones seem to shake. But then you hear it. The soft, desperate wailing. And you realize that is why your soul grows cold. That is why every part of you wants to leave and never return. That is what becomes of the souls broken by a dark practitioner. They are the cold misery of Hel.*

I recoiled from his words. *Is there nothing we can do to help them?*

No, Sigrun said evenly. *All we can do is release them from this form before they can cause more harm. They will kill anything they come across. They can only be controlled by whoever summoned them, and no one creates the draugr with good intentions. There is no healing the damage done to their souls.*

How? Mikhail asked. *Will beheading them work?*

No. Sigrun shook her head. *We must find the item they're bonded to and destroy it. It's likely deeper in the cave, but we need to break them apart first so they don't come after us. If the seidr dark practitioner is still here, they will draw the draugr back to them to use against us. We need to neutralize them here so we can continue our search.*

Hack and slash, boys. Nemain smiled grimly as she stared at the dozens of draugr beneath us. *We have to break their bodies apart into pieces and scatter those pieces as much as we can.*

How do you know all this? Mikhail asked Nemain.

That's for me to know and you not to. She smirked. Mikhail narrowed his eyes at her but refrained from arguing further.

Nemain looked at us, her no-nonsense mask falling into place. *All of you stay up here. We'll handle this. Under no circumstances are you to go down there, do you understand?* She waited until we all nodded. I wanted to argue that I could be helpful but based on Nemain's expression I suspected she would open a gateway and shove us all threw it if we pushed her on this.

Good. Gunnar and Viggo will keep an eye on you, Nemain said once we'd all promised to obey her command.

I didn't think it was possible for a cat to truly sneer, but Viggo proved me wrong. To my surprise, he didn't argue but simply curled up into a ball and closed his eyes. Gunnar studied the napping skogkatt and let out a soft sigh before lying down on his haunches near the ledge where he could keep an eye on the draugr below. Apparently, the white wolf took his order of guarding us seriously.

Nemain pulled her twin blades free in a fast, practiced motion and leapt down to the cavern below. The draugr stopped their shuffling and slowly turned their heads towards where Nemain crouched, her head bowed, as if in prayer. Magos and Mikhail moved towards the ledge, but Sigrun held out her arms, blocking them from joining Nemain. *Give her a minute. She needs this.*

I flinched as ear-splitting shrieks tore out of the draugr before the ones close to Nemain leapt towards her. Elisa sucked in a breath next to me, and I understood her surprise completely. The draugr moved so fast they were almost a blur. I'd assumed they would be slow to attack based on how they'd been shuffling around the cave floor, but apparently they could be fast as hell when they wanted to be. Nemain's blades whirled, and the first wave of draugr fell, their heads and bodies going in different directions.

Elisa tugged me down, and I sat on the ledge beside her, Damon sitting on my other side and Misha sitting next to Elisa. We watched in stunned silence as Nemain cut her way through the draugr like it was a dance. A sound echoed through the cavern, and it took me a moment to realize it was Nemain laughing. Blue flames occasionally flickered on her blades as she hacked apart the draugr piece by piece.

This was a side of Nemain I'd never seen before, and it unsettled me a little. She was always a little wild when she sparred, and I knew what she was capable of. Or at least I thought I did. But seeing her now... there was such an edge of violence to how she moved. Like she reveled in the chaos she was causing. It didn't change how I felt about her, not truly. She was still my friend and I trusted her with my life and Finn's. But I understood now why there was often fear and wariness behind the eyes of others when they saw her coming.

Over half of the draugr lay broken on the ground when movement from the other side of the cave caught my eye. "What is that?" I said out loud without thinking, as parts of the cave wall seemed to peel away. It was too dark to see what was happening, but I could just make out two large forms lumbering to the large open space where Nemain was still unleashing herself on the draugr. Both forms stomped down the slope, causing the floor beneath us to rumble.

"There you are," Sigrun said, as if she expected this.

"What are they?" My eyes stayed locked on the two hulking creatures. Their dark grey skin blended into the walls of the cave, and I wondered if they'd been there this whole time. They had to be at least ten feet tall, and I couldn't even begin to guess how much they weighed. They looked like freaking boulders come to life. Long arms ending in blunt hands dragged on the ground, and they stared at Nemain with cloudy white eyes beneath thick brows.

"Some type of cave troll. These ones are native to this realm. The draugr don't interest them because they're dead, and the trolls don't eat things that are dead." Sigrun explained.

"Eat?" Damon asked uncertainly.

Sigrun ignored him. "I was hoping we wouldn't run into any of them. They usually hide deeper in the caves and only come out at night." Here eyes fell to where Nemain was still busy cutting through the draugr.

"Vampires, take the one on the left. I'll get the other one. Go for the heart." The valkyrie launched herself off the ledge and slammed shield first into one of the trolls. Her golden wings snapped open as the troll stumbled back a step, shaking its large head several times before leaning forward and bellowing in rage. It tried to grab Sigrun out of the air, but unlike the draugr, it was every bit as slow as it looked, and she easily dodged. The troll chased after Sigrun as she led it away from Nemain, who was still busy cutting apart the draugr, trusting the others to deal with the trolls.

Just as the other troll got within striking distance of Nemain, Magos and Mikhail vanished in puffs of mists, reappearing a second later above the troll. They pierced the eyes of the troll at the same time before once again turning to mist and landing several feet away. The blinded troll screamed in rage and flung its hands around like sledgehammers, knocking aside the draugr that were too close and sending them crashing into the wall.

Nemain swung her blade at a draugr the troll had missed just as it changed its direction and hammered its fist straight down. Mikhail grabbed her and pulled her back as the fist slammed the draugr into the ground.

"Gross," Damon said as he stared at the flattened draugr that was still twitching.

"I mean, there's no blood or guts, really," Misha argued. "It's not that gross."

"Do you think they have anything on the inside?" I asked, squinting at the draugr parts strewn about the floor. We were too far away, and the light was too dim for me to see anything.

"The only thing I see coming out of them is dust and

bone." Elisa scrunched up her nose. "I wonder if that's because these were all made from old corpses or if that's simply what the magic does to their bodies."

A violent shake tore through the cave as the troll Sigrun had been fighting fell, the valkyrie holding up a large heart covered in dark blood before throwing it at us. Damon let out a shriek and raised his arms, but Gunnar snatched the heart out of the air, dark green blood splattering against his pristine white coat. Viggo snickered, and Damon glared at him.

Troll hearts are one of Gunnar's favorites. He doesn't get them that often, since there aren't many trolls outside the Yggdrasil and fae realms.

I looked at Gunnar in time to see him tear a chunk off the heart and raise his muzzle as he chewed on it, pure ecstasy on his face. *Gross.*

"Okay," Misha said as he stared at Gunnar in disgust. "I could have done without seeing that, but the rest of this trip has been awesome so far. I'm so glad we got out of the apartment for this." Elisa and Damon nodded in agreement as they watched Magos deliver the fatal blow to the remaining troll. Mikhail and Sigrun had joined Nemain in hacking apart the fallen draugr and flinging their body parts around.

With a start I noticed that Jinx was no longer perched on the ledge. I scanned the chaos below trying to see where the grimalkin had disappeared to. I saw a dark flash and then he crashed into the center of a draugr causing it to slam into the ground. I felt a pulse of magic and then pieces of the draugr flew outward as if pulled by some imaginary force.

"What the hell?" I stared at Jinx in bewilderment when he did it again.

"Huh," Elisa said casually, as if seeing a relatively small feline break apart bodies in seconds was a normal thing. "Didn't know he could do that."

Less than a quarter of the draugr remained. I still itched to be down their fighting, but Nemain had given us an order and

I would obey it. I took note of the methods that her and the others were using to dispatch the draugr for future reference. Although I hoped to never encounter them again. It still bothered me greatly what had been done to their souls.

The vampires continued debating the grossness of the situation while I studied Sigrun. I didn't think she was going to hold to her only three days proclamation, but I had no doubt she was still planning on sending us packing as soon as this situation was sorted out. Which meant I didn't have much time to change her mind about mentoring me, and I still had no idea how to accomplish that.

"I need your help." I interrupted Damon's speech about why the dusty insides of the draugr were, in fact, disgusting, and all three of them looked at me. "All of you. I need help from all of you."

"Okay," Misha said slowly. "To do what?"

"Change Sigrun's mind about mentoring me. Not only for my sake, but for hers too. It's not right that she's all alone here."

"Maybe she likes it," Damon said. "I personally would love some alone time." Elisa smacked the back of his head, and he winced while he rubbed it. "Just saying, a little peace and quiet is nice."

"I'm not saying we need to convince her to move in with us." There wasn't space in the apartment building, anyway. "Just agree to let me visit on a regular basis. And the others." I gestured at Magos, Mikhail, and Nemain. "She doesn't want to admit it, but Sigrun has enjoyed having all of us here."

"True," Elisa murmured. "I don't fully understand her reluctance to teach you. If you were involved with the rest of the valkyries, I would understand, but you're not. Being your mentor wouldn't require her to interact with them again. There must be some other reason she's holding back."

We all gazed down at Sigrun, who was currently arguing

with Nemain over something while Mikhail, Magos and Jinx continued to spread out the broken pieces of the draugr more. I could still feel the off-putting magic pulsing as it struggled to put the draugr back together.

"Maybe Nemain can help us figure it out?" Damon suggested.

"I think Nemain wants to help Sigrun, but her people skills aren't exactly . . . ummm . . . the best." I winced as Nemain shoved Sigrun hard and Magos had to step in-between them. "Her method of getting Sigrun to agree is probably going to involve a sword somehow, and I don't think that's going to help. That's probably what she's been doing for their entire history based on how they've been acting around each other."

"I'll try to get Magos alone and ask him about it," Elisa said. "He doesn't know Sigrun all that well, but he might know something about Nemain's history with her that would be useful."

A soft rustling sound came from behind us, and we all turned quickly to face it only to find nothing there. Misha crept forward and peered down the tunnel we had come through before turning to face us again with a shrug. "Nothing there."

I stared at the space where I thought I had seen a flash of brown fur but saw nothing more.

"Y'all ready?" Nemain called up from the cavern floor.

"Yep!" We immediately chimed back.

"We'll keep going." Sigrun eyed the dark tunnel at the other side of the cavern from where we sat. "There are more open spaces like this one further in. I can feel the traces of seidr magic, we need to find whatever the object the draugr are bonded with and destroy it."

"Why are they here?" I asked. "Why would a dark practitioner of seidr send them to this realm?"

"That doesn't concern you," Sigrun said coldly. "If I had it my way, all of you would gone right now." She shot Nemain an irritated look, the shifter just smiled causing a red sheen to flash over Sigrun's eyes before she focused on me once more. "It's my business and I'll handle it. If things get too dangerous, Nemain *will* open a gateway and get you all out of here."

Before I or Nemain could argue, Sigrun slipped into the tunnels, the glowing orbs trailed after her. I took in a deep breath and then flew across the cavern. I waited a few seconds before heading into the tunnel. I'd give Sigrun a little time to cool off, but then it was time for us to have a chat about what the hell was going on here.

Chapter Twelve

Can we speak out loud? I asked Sigrun as we traveled further into the cave system. With each step, it felt like she was putting up a wall between us, and I was doing my best not to panic and attempt to tear it down. I needed to go about this carefully, and that meant patience.

Mikhail was walking ahead of us with Damon, while the rest were behind us. I couldn't hear or see Magos, and I suspected Elisa was doing her best to get any information out of him.

Already tired of speaking mind-to-mind? Sigrun asked. Her tone held no judgment, and she didn't spare so much as a glance in my direction.

A little, I said, and it was true. A dull ache was forming behind my eyes. I hoped this wouldn't happen every time I used telepathy.

"We can talk openly," Sigrun said. "The draugr usually stick to their group, so we shouldn't encounter any more, and it will take them at least a few hours to piece themselves together again. If the practitioner is still in this realm, they would have felt us break apart their toys and therefore know where we are."

Sigrun stepped to the side to allow Gunnar to pass through. The white wolf moved to walk next to Damon, who absently reached out and stroked the wolf's fur. He probably did it without thinking, so used to Elisa's wolf. I held my breath, half expecting Gunnar to snap at the vampire's touch, but he only moved closer, giving Damon better access.

"You'll need to practice speaking telepathically more," Sigrun continued. "Add it to the list of things you'll need to work on once you leave here."

"Of course," I said, nodding deeply. Out of the corner of my eye, I saw Sigrun turn her head towards me. She was probably wondering why I was being so agreeable all of a sudden. I continued to stare ahead at Gunnar, my neutral mask firmly in place.

"Bryn—" Sigrun started, but I quickly cut her off.

"Who do you think this practitioner is?" I asked. "Do all of the Vanir have a problem with you?"

"There are many in the Yggdrasil realms who have a problem with me. I move every so often, but they always find me eventually. It's been a while since one of them has bothered to find my new home and pay me a visit. Perhaps they felt they were overdue," Sigrun hedged.

Bullshit. I inwardly flinched, hoping she hadn't caught my thoughts. When Sigrun didn't comment, I assumed Damon had dropped the link between us or she was choosing to ignore it. "Yggdrasil realms? Those are the nine realms that are all linked together right? Niflheim, Musplheim, Asgard, Vanaheim, Jotunheim, Svartalfheim, Helheim, Alfheim, and Midgard," I recounted, being careful to get the pronunciations right but it was hard.

"Eight realms," Sigrun corrected. "Midgard is the human

realm, and it was never truly a part of Yggdrasil, despite what some believed. Given that you spent most of your life in a fae realm, I'm assuming you're familiar with how natural gateways are formed?"

"Sort of." I frowned. "The fae I grew up with didn't talk about it all that often. They just accepted the existence of multiple realms and moved on. But I've spent some time at Pele's bar, and Asmodeus talked to me about it. They have an interest in studying the creation and history of the realms."

"Many of the daemons do. The dwarves of Svartalfheim do as well, and many other species. It's only the fae who have zero interest in understanding how our many realms came to be."

"The fae only care about magic and little of history," I said with a snort.

"I don't believe I've ever met Asmodeus. What did they tell you?"

"Most of it was over my head, to be honest," I admitted. I considered myself a fairly smart person prior to meeting Asmodeus. After a thirty-minute conversation with them, I felt like a child learning my letters. Still, the conversation had been enlightening, and Asmodeus was kind and patient.

"They said the realms were likely alternative realities that had split apart long ago and now exist as parallel universes, and new ones are still being born that we simply haven't discovered yet. All of these parallel universes exist within the same space. . . The how and why of that is where things got a bit fuzzy for me. We call these alternative realties realms. When a new one is born, it has a stronger connection to the one it split off from than other realms, and sometimes the walls between those particular realms are weak and gateways can form. The fae have many realms because several of them split off from the same original one, which resulted in a lot of these natural gateways."

"This Asmodeus seems like a smart person. You would do well to continue learning from them.

"Yggdrasil is similar to all the fae realms. The eight realms all have gateways between them and have since the beginning. Much later in our history, natural gateways formed between our realms and the human realm, which we called Midgard. But this wasn't special. Many natural gateways formed within the human realm because of the amount of magic it contains. Since the fae and daemons worked to put the protective guards around their realms and the human one to protect it from the devourers, these natural gateways no longer form, and the existing ones were mostly closed. The Aesir and Vanir bargained with the fae to keep the gateways open between the rest of the realms of Yggdrasil and the human realm."

I started to ask why they had bothered to bargain to keep access to the human realm, but then I realized Sigrun was deliberately steering the conversation away from my original question. She was using my obvious interest in learning more about Yggdrasil to avoid taking about her history. And I'd fallen for it.

"Is it specifically those from Vanaheim who have targeted you over the years?" I asked, redirecting the conversation once more.

The muscles along Sigrun's jaw tensed at my question. "Not always."

"Who else?" I pushed.

"It's mostly those from Vanaheim and Asgard," she said begrudgingly. "The Jötnar, elves, and dwarves stay out of my business."

"Do the other valkyries still come after you?"

"Not anymore," Sigrun said coldly, but I could hear the echo of pain in her voice.

I let the silence fall between us again, unsure how to

proceed. If I pushed too hard, Sigrun would shut down completely.

Elisa says to give Sigrun a few minutes and then steer the conversation back to the Vanir and who this dark practitioner might be, Damon said quietly in my mind. *She's speaking with Magos now and getting some ideas about how to proceed.*

Okay. I pushed the thought out. The dull ache in my head was starting to ease, but even that small word caused me to flinch as a sharp pain struck behind my eyes. I would need to practice in small amounts of time when we got back to build up my tolerance for communicating like this.

The white coat of Gunnar disappeared as he turned around the bend in the cave, and I heard a soft gasp from Damon. We entered another large cavern. This one was full of odd formations that spiraled from the ceiling to the floor. In-between all these spirals were silken strands that formed intricate designs that gave off a soft blue glow. It was like stepping into another world, and I found myself slowly moving through the cavern, taking it all in. Moisture had collected on the strands, and where the droplets joined together, the glowing was brighter, like tiny stars.

"What are they?" Elisa asked in awe.

"Silkworms," Sigrun said. "I've found caverns like this before, always deep within a cave system. Their silk gives off some sort of bioluminescence."

I stepped towards the webbing, careful not to disturb it, and saw tiny green worms inching their way among the silken strands. They were smaller than my thumbnail and easy to miss. "They remind me of the pixies back home. They would gather in fields when certain flowers were in bloom and light up the night sky."

"This is one of the many hidden treasures of this realm," Sigrun said from where she stood in front of a particularly large and intricate web. "Their colors vary based on region.

Further south they give off a soft orange glow and to the east they're an electric green."

"I would love to see that. Finn would enjoy it, too."

Sigrun said nothing. I couldn't help the disappointment that struck me. She didn't think I or Finn would have ever the chance to see that. I wasn't making any progress in changing her mind about training me. *Patience*, I told myself. There was still time left.

We stayed in the cavern, watching the small worms move about their never-ending task of spinning more silk until Nemain urged us onward. Reluctantly, we followed after Sigrun and Nemain as they continued down another tunnel. Elisa fell into step with Magos once again behind us, and I was surprised when Mikhail joined me.

"How goes your attempts to change Sigrun's mind? Have Elisa and the others come up with any helpful ideas?"

"You know?" I asked in surprise. Mikhail and I hadn't spent much time together since I'd come to stay with Nemain. He had been with Nemain when they'd found me and had helped in my rescue from the fae who were after me and Finn, but since returning to the human realm, I had rarely spoken with him.

Mikhail arched a dark eyebrow at me. "Former assassin, remember? Plus, I survived for a long time living amongst the sharks of the Vampire Council. I know plotting when I see it."

"You make it sound so nefarious," I whispered. "Sigrun needs our help."

"A valkyrie warrior who has seen over a thousand years come and go needs the help of four teenagers?"

Annoyance flickered through me even as a blush ran up my neck. I really wished I didn't blush so easily every time I was flustered. It was getting tiresome. "I'm twenty and Elisa is nineteen. We're not teenagers."

"You should be glad I didn't call you children."

"I'm beginning to understand why Nemain finds you so annoying."

"She finds me annoying for a very different reason." Mikhail grinned. He wasn't my type, but even I had to admit he was awfully pretty with his blend of masculine and feminine features. His dark eyes held a hint of something dangerous and wild, which made me wary, but I suspected appealed to Nemain. Not that she was likely to admit *that* anytime soon. "I understand why Elisa sought out Magos for help in this. She hopes to learn more about Nemain's history with Sigrun and glean useful information from that. Plus, Elisa and the others grew up under the loving care of the Council, and my previous profession makes them uncomfortable."

"They trust you," I said quietly. "I know I'm new to this group, and I'm still learning about all of you. But you should know that despite your past allegiance to the Council, they trust you now. You just make them a little nervous sometimes because you're . . . well . . . you." I waved my hand at the various weapons he had strapped to his body.

Mikhail swallowed and didn't say anything for a moment. "Despite being cast out by her people, Sigrun still believes in their ways. They may have turned their backs on her, but if they called for aid, she would answer. She probably wishes she could cast aside her honor, but like my uncle, Sigrun is honorable to a fault. It is both her greatest strength and her greatest weakness."

"You barely know her. What makes you so sure?"

Mikhail's dark hair fell over his shoulder as he shrugged. "I'm excellent at identifying weaknesses in others. It's why I was so valuable to the Council all those years. Anyone can learn how to kill others quickly and efficiently. I excelled at finding what makes others vulnerable and exploiting that for information or to bend them to my will, and thus the Council's will."

This was the side of Mikhail that unsettled Elisa and the others, and I understood why as I fought to keep the revulsion off my face. Part of me wanted to ask what exactly Mikhail had done to help the Vampire Council in their war against the werewolves all those years, but another part wanted to walk away from him and never speak of it again. But I refused to live in ignorance, even if it was the easier path.

I continued to walk by him, thinking through what he had said. He wouldn't have brought this up for no reason. Why would Sigrun's loyalty to the valkyries keep her from helping me?

"What do you think the other valkyries would do if they learned I existed and Sigrun was my mentor?" I asked, a suspicion tickling the back of my mind. Mikhail didn't answer, but a small smile played across his lips, and I knew I was on the right track. "I already have a strike against me because of my bond with Finn. They might be willing to overlook that, but if they knew that I was also training with Sigrun, that I was friends with her. . ." My brows furrowed as I thought about the implications. The valkyries would assume Sigrun told me at least some of her history about what had happened to her bonded. They feared what Sigrun had done and what would happen if others followed suit. If I destroyed my bonded the way that Sigrun had hers, I would become a powerful valkyrie, quite possibly the most powerful. And I would have no allegiance the valkyries.

I would never harm Finn, so that possibility would never happen. But the other valkyries didn't know me. They would likely only see the potential threat. "She's trying to protect me," I whispered.

"Yes." Mikhail nodded approvingly. "She's not foolish. She knows just as I did that you're plotting something. As soon as we leave this realm, she'll likely move somewhere else where you can't find her."

Coldness ran through me. I didn't want to be the reason Sigrun left her home and went even further into seclusion. I had to change her mind. "How do I fix this?" The question was more to myself than Mikhail, but he answered anyway.

"No idea. I just wanted to make sure you were working on the right problem. Now if you'll excuse me, I'm going to go see if I can annoy Nemain enough to get her to throw a dagger at me."

I blinked. "There's something very wrong with you."

Mikhail winked at me and sauntered further ahead to where Nemain was leading the group.

Seconds later, Elisa silently appeared next to me, and I jumped slightly. "I really wish you all would stop doing that."

"We know." She grinned and for a moment all the troubled thoughts in my head went on hiatus as my heart skipped a beat. "Did Mikhail have anything useful to give us about our Sigrun problem?"

"You knew that's what we were talking about?"

"Nothing gets past Mikhail. That vampire sees everything. I knew that if I sought out Magos, he would think we were on the wrong track and would intervene. I actually thought he would find me afterwards. I was a little surprised he went directly to you."

"You're incredibly hot right now." The words slipped out before I could claw them back, and I turned a lovely shade of red.

Elisa smiled wider. "I know."

I filled Elisa in on what Mikhail had told me, and she shared what little information Magos had been able to give her. Sigrun had disappeared in the past and gone to places where even Nemain couldn't find her. "I have to change her mind today," I said. "Otherwise she'll leave, and I might never find her again. We're running out of time."

Elisa's hand slipped into mine. "We'll figure it out." That

odd sense of wrongness swept through me again, and I stopped mid-step. It felt like bugs crawling across my skin, and my magic was vibrating violently within me in response. "What is it?" Elisa asked, immediately going on alert.

Ahead of us, Sigrun flexed her wings, light dimly reflecting off her golden feathers. She must have felt it, too. "I think we've found the practitioner."

Chapter Thirteen

"Come out, come out, wherever you are." The words echoed down the tunnel along with a wave of foul magic that made my skin crawl.

Sigrun flared her wings open before snapping them in tight and stalking off towards the voice. Silently, we all followed after her. I was envious of the vampires who couldn't see or really sense magic. The closer we got to the source of the voice, the more it felt like the dark magic was coating my skin. I had to force myself to keep my hands at my sides instead of scratching at my arms. Even the light from the orbs that floated above us had changed to a dark sickly green color in reaction to the seidr magic.

We rounded another corner, and I was surprised to see light pouring in ahead. I blinked rapidly, trying to adjust to the brightness as Sigrun led us into a large, open cavern. The space was easily triple the size of the area where we had fought the draugr, and the ground was level. I glanced up and saw large holes in the cave ceiling, as if a giant had pierced it repeatedly with a spear. Golden afternoon sunlight shot to the cave floor, and hovering in-between those beams was a young woman with fiery red hair and pale skin. She smiled as we entered the cavern, spreading out in front of her with our backs to the wall.

That beautiful smile was a thing of nightmares. It contained no joy or life, just emptiness. Like the magic wrapping around me, everything about it just screamed wrong. Her eyes had a cloudy white coloring that hid whatever their original color had been. The black paint that had been brushed across the bridge of her nose and eyes only made them stand out more. Lines were also painted down her body. She wore no clothing, jewelry, or weapons.

Only magic.

Unlike the magic I felt swirling around me, this magic I could see. It shimmered across her skin, casting off a dark green glow, sending out thin whispering strands which rattled me every time they brushed against my skin. She looked so young. I knew the Vanir could live for centuries, some longer, if they had enough magic, but they did age. It was possible she was older than she appeared, but something told me she truly was my age.

"What's wrong with her?" Elisa asked, two curved daggers in her hands.

"She's a vessel," Sigrun said, not taking her eyes off the Vanir girl. "Someone is possessing her, probably the same someone who brought the draugr here."

"Why isn't she attacking us?" I asked. The axe was still strapped to my back. I should have taken it off before we'd entered the cavern, but I hadn't been thinking straight. The seidr magic had bothered me during the draugr encounter, but it was nothing like this. My skin still crawled, and my magic was building inside me, grinding against my bones. Unhooking axe still felt foreign to me, and I couldn't do it quickly; I was worried I would draw her attention if I tried.

Milky eyes focused on me, and I forced myself to not take a

step back. "Because I wanted to talk to you first, beautiful one," she said.

Sigrun launched herself into the air but was immediately ripped back down by thick black vines that sprang out of the earth. Nemain fell on the vines, hacking chunks of them away, but more took their place and wrapped around the shifter. She hissed in rage, trying to cut her way free as Mikhail joined her. Together they tried to cut Sigrun out but there were too many and soon they were both covered. Dark purple thorns shot out and they screamed as those thorns cut into their flesh. Mist formed around Mikhail, only to roll off his skin.

"Magos, don't let the vines grab you!" I screamed, but it was too late. Damon dodged one that erupted from the earth, only to get entangled with another. Magos's hand shot out to block the one that struck at the young vampire's throat, and the thorns bit into him. He bellowed in pain and fell to his knees as more vines wrapped around him. I spun to help Misha but found he was already pinned against the wall. In less than a minute, this slip of a Vanir girl had neutralized most of our group.

Elisa sliced through the dark strands that tried to wrap around her, nimbly dancing away from the reach of others. More seidr magic pulsed from the girl, and I ran towards Elisa. Gunnar was faster than me. The white wolf slammed into Elisa's chest, kicking out with his back feet. She flew backwards as a dozen vines sprang up to capture the wolf. I reached her side a moment later, and we both panted.

I quickly scanned the cavern, trying to locate Viggo and Jinx, but didn't see them anywhere. Either they had managed to avoid being captured, or they were in the thorny bundle that contained Mikhail, Sigrun, and Nemain. Vines shot up around us but made no move to attack. One slithered across the ground towards Elisa, and she slapped her foot down on it. As it writhed beneath her heel, another shot towards her face, and she sliced it in half.

The Vanir girl laughed as I stared at Elisa with both eyebrows raised. I had no idea she was that good with knives.

"No touching," Elisa warned.

"How adorable," the Vanir crooned. The wrongness of her voice made the hairs on the back of my neck standup. It didn't match the young girl hovering above us; it was too rich and confident. "You got yourself a little vampire protector."

I was feeling vastly out of my depth, but I forced the rising panic down. Losing my shit wouldn't help anyone. So far, all the vines were doing was containing everyone else and blocking them from using their magic.

Whoever this dark practitioner was, she wanted to speak with me. I might as well get information from her while Nemain and the others broke free. And I had no doubt they would. My energy would be better spent collecting information than attempting to free them. If I took a single step towards them, I'd find myself wrapped up and unable to move.

"Who are you?" By some miracle, my voice came out calm and even, despite the rapid beating of my heart.

The Vanir floated closer to me. Elisa tensed but made no move to strike at her. She stopped a few feet away from us, still hovering above the ground. This close, she was even younger than I thought. Her face still had traces of baby fat and held the innocence of youth, except for her eyes. They were ancient and cruel.

"I am power. I am the rightful ruler of the Yggdrasil realms. I am someone to be worshipped." She nimbly ran her fingers down her body. "This young one was one of my most devout worshippers. It will be a shame to lose her, but sacrifices must be made."

"Let me be more clear," I said tightly. "What is your name? And what do you want?"

"I want many things." A coy smile played across the girl's lips. "But right now I want you."

"Why?" Fear skittered across my skin. Nothing good could come from a dark seidr practitioner taking an interest in me.

"Your presence here is quite fortuitous," she said, ignoring my question. "I had to alter my plans slightly to give us this opportunity to speak. I can offer you so much more than the broken valkyrie."

Wisps of magic floated off her and stroked my cheek. I stilled at the touch, the fear I'd been feeling slipped away as heat and pleasure swept through me. A small part of me recoiled at the feeling of the dark seidr magic brushing against my skin, but I lost myself in the promise of it.

I could protect Finn and everyone I cared about.

I would never be too slow or too weak again.

I would be powerful.

Yes, a deep sultry voice echoed in my mind. My feet inched forward another step. *Come with me.*

Another step.

A bone-rattling scream snapped me out of it, and I stumbled back. The Vanir girl hovered a dozen feet away, her hand wrapped around the dagger that had pierced her right eye.

"Stay away from her, you creepy bitch!" Elisa snarled, raising her remaining dagger.

My magic rallied, and I slammed my mental walls back up. I hadn't realized I'd let them down, and the practitioner had used the opening to sink her claws into me. Later I would be pissed at myself for making such a foolish mistake, but for now we just needed to survive. I pulled my axe free and moved to stand next to Elisa. The Vanir yanked the dagger out, blood pouring from the empty eye socket. It didn't show any signs of healing. Either the practitioner couldn't heal whatever body she possessed or she had exhausted too much of her magic summoning the vines.

Good for us. Bad for her.

"Someday soon I'm going to carve your vampire lover apart in front of you," she said matter-of-factly, as if announcing she would be dropping by for lunch next week. Icy rage shot through me, followed quickly by panic at the thought of Elisa being harmed. My grip on the axe tightened as Gunnar let out a low whine. The Vanir glanced back at the thorns still covering Nemain and Sigrun and tilted her head to the side. "What is tha—"

Blue flames exploded out of the vines, engulfing them in an instant. Nemain stood, bathed in blood and her ghostly blue flames as the vines crumbled away in ashes and frost. Sigrun shot into the sky, eyes glowing red and her axe pulled back. The Vanir girl smiled eerily as Sigrun swung and the girl's head toppled to the floor. The body continued to hover for a few seconds before it fell with a thud and the remaining vines burst in puffs of green light. The last remains of dark seidr magic faded from the cavern. All that remained was the broken body of the Vanir girl.

Misha and Damon fell forward from the wall they'd been pinned against, and Gunnar sprang to his feet. A relieved breath burst from my lips at seeing everyone still alive and in more or less one piece. Nemain was running her hands over Magos, her eyes tight with concern. He gently clasped her hands and pulled them away.

"I'm fine," he said. "Your magic didn't hurt me. It didn't hurt any of us."

"Okay." A shuddering breath tore out of Nemain, and she nodded, her ashen hair falling loosely around her face. "Okay," she repeated before walking away and vanishing down one of the tunnels.

"She just needs a minute," Elisa said quietly to me. "Nemain doesn't like to use that part of her magic. She always fears she's going to hurt someone she cares about."

We watched as Magos moved to join Sigrun who was studying the body of the Vanir girl, while Mikhail gazed down the tunnel where Nemain had disappeared. He took a few steps towards it but stopped, hesitation flashing across his face before he moved forward, as if pulled by a rope, and headed down the tunnel after Nemain.

"Do we think he'll be okay?" Misha asked worriedly. "Nemain's not exactly in the best frame of mind right now, and Mikhail does have a tendency to push her buttons."

The vampire will be fine, Jinx said as he trotted into the room with something dangling from his mouth.

"Where have you been?" I asked, thinking back to before the vines had exploded from the ground. Neither of the felines had been present. "Is Viggo with you?"

No. The skogkatt appeared in front of me. His tufted ears swiveling back and forth. *I never left.*

"And you didn't think to help us?" I stared at him incredulously.

I was biding my time. Viggo sniffed, raising his nose in the air.

More like being a waste of space as usual, Jinx replied. *I, however, actually did something useful and tracked down the item the draugr were bonded to.* He dropped a necklace on the ground. Several carved wooden tiles were attached to a thin twine of rope that was knotted together.

"That's it?" I peered down at the necklace. A faint pulse of magic came from it, but it was barely noticeable. If I hadn't been looking for it, I never would have sensed it. "How in the world did you find it?"

Talent, Jinx said at the same time Viggo said, *Fae bullshit.*

The felines glared at each other, and Gunnar smoothly stepped between them. I couldn't help but smile in amusement at the wolf. A fierce and powerful predator, playing peacekeeper between two egotistical cats.

Sigrun ignored them as she swiped the necklace off the

ground, a troubled expression on her face. "Nemain," she called out, not bothering to raise her voice. With her shapeshifter hearing, Nemain would hear her as long as she hadn't gone too far. Even if she didn't, Mikhail definitely would.

Less than a minute later, Nemain swept into the cavern with the vampire trailing her. Nemain bore a look of indifference which I knew meant she was feeling too much still and was shutting it down. Mikhail had a similar expression, but I didn't know him well enough to know what that meant. I didn't see any fresh signs of blood on either of them, and their clothing wasn't anymore disheveled than it had been when they'd left the cavern earlier. I slid a glance at Elisa, and she just smirked and shrugged a shoulder.

Sigrun tossed the necklace to Nemain who snatched it out of the air. "I don't have my supplies with me to destroy it properly. But you can."

Nemain stared at the necklace like it would bite her and slowly raised her eyes to meet Sigrun's. The valkyrie merely arched an eyebrow in challenge. She wanted Nemain to use her devourer magic again, I realized. The shifter had gone predatory still, and I couldn't help the unsettling chill that ran through me. It disturbed me when Nemain and the vampires did that. It was a reminder of just how different they were from us. Valkyries, daemons, fae, we were all dangerous. But something was distinctly different about the species that were predators first and people second. It was easy to forget because of how they acted most of the time, but moments like this made it impossible to ignore.

Instead of backing down, Sigrun smiled broadly at Nemain. Dear gods, she was insane.

"Maybe we should—" I jumped back quickly with a yelp as blue fire shot up from Nemain's palm and engulfed the necklace. The flames writhed from Nemain as if they had a life of their own. Viggo scrambled back, but Sigrun held her ground, even as the flames brushed against her chest and arms.

Just as suddenly as they appeared, the flames receded into Nemain, and she tilted her hand, letting the frozen ashes fall to the ground. Jinx, who hadn't moved during the fiery display, quickly stepped to the side to avoid the ashes falling into his fur.

"You're never going to learn how to control it if you're too scared to use it," Sigrun said.

Nemain laughed coldly. "You're one to talk of fear, valkyrie. After hiding in this realm for centuries."

"Nemain," I warned. "Now isn't the time."

"That's just it, Bryn. It's never the time for Sigrun. I've given her space. I brought her to this bloody realm." Nemain's green eyes seemed to glow as her rage increased. "I've respected her goddamn wishes. And the one time I come to her and ask for something, she says no!" Nemain finished somewhere between a growl and a roar. Sigrun had pushed her too far, and Nemain was shoving back hard. Frantically I turned towards Elisa for help, but she appeared just as panicked as I felt.

Magos's lips were pursed and his eyes flooded with concern, but he made no move to intervene. And Mikhail, the bastard, was grinning like he was pleased someone else was bearing the brunt of Nemain's anger. *Shit, shit, shit.* I needed more time to change Sigrun's mind, and if she and Nemain got into an all-out fight, I would lose my chance. *Think, Bryn, think.* I needed to take their attention off each other.

"It doesn't make sense," I blurted out. Both Sigrun and Nemain turned their rage-filled eyes towards me, and I quickly continued before I lost my opening. "That girl . . . or whoever . . . whatever that was, she went through all that effort and for what? After she restrained all of you, she said she wanted to talk to me. But she was in this realm before we arrived. She was here for something else and only spoke to me because I happened to be here. But why spend all this magic to bring the draugr here and put on this big display of seidr magic?"

"To draw me out. We're far from my home," Sigrun murmured. "Even if I flew as fast as I could, it would take me hours to make it back." The rage that had been pouring off her moments ago was fading. I held in the sigh of relief I wanted so desperately to let out.

"They didn't know we would be here." Nemain frowned. "They didn't know I would be here, and you would have a way of getting home fast." She extended a hand, and instead of blue flames shooting out, the air rippled slightly. Nemain's brow furrowed in concentrated, and Sigrun peered around her shoulder to see the gateway struggling to open. I moved to stand next to Sigrun as we watched Nemain slowly feed more of her magic into the gateway. Finally, it snapped open, revealing Sigrun's cottage.

"That's new," the valkyrie said in surprise. "At least you've been practicing with *some* of your magic."

Enough, I thought. Before I could think better of it, I slammed my foot down on the valkyrie's. She let out a hiss of pain and stared at me in shock before throwing her head back and letting out a deep laugh. Nemain looked at her and then at me. I gave her a sheepish smile and tried in vain to keep the blush off my face. A chuckle spilled out of Nemain, and soon she was laughing so hard she had to wipe the tears from her eyes.

"Come on then," Nemain said between laughs. "Let's go see if we can figure out what that practitioner asshole was after."

Chapter Fourteen

I SCANNED the outside of the cottage and workshop warily as everyone passed through the gateway. Several loud clangs came from the workshop, and I took a step forward, but Sigrun's outstretched arm stopped me from going to investigate. Nobody had drawn their weapons, and I followed their lead, leaving my axe strapped to my back and my shield contained to the bracelet on my wrist. The clanging stopped, and the sudden silence felt wrong. I realized all the birds that had been flitting between the tall stalks of grass the last time we'd been there were quiet. Even the buzz of the insects had died down, as if all the local critters knew unwelcome guests were in their realm.

"You might as well come out," Sigrun called. "You won't like it if I have to drag you out."

Three beings exited the workshop and strode towards us, their pace confident and unhurried. The tallest one was a female, and she looked a few inches short of five feet with a sturdy muscular build one only got from manual labor. Her wine red hair was pulled back in elaborate braids and freckles were smattered across her face, if not for the scowl she might have been pretty. The two males who followed her wore matching scowls, but their red hair was closely cropped to their heads. They stopped twenty feet away from us. The female's eyes never left Sigrun, but the males were quickly assessing all of us, their frowns deepening.

I'd have to confirm with Sigrun later, but I assumed these were dwarves from Svartalfheim. They must have been working with the seidr practitioner, which I thought odd. It was my understanding from the little research I'd done and from chatting with Sigrun these past couple of days that the dwarves didn't like the Vanir anymore than they did the Aesir and usually avoided them both.

The back door to the cottage banged open, and two more dwarves joined the other three, one male, one female. They also had dark red hair, but these two had pulled their hair back into tight buns. I wondered if they were all related or if this was just a common hair color amongst dwarves. All five dwarves eyed us suspiciously, but none of them drew the weapons they had strapped to their backs and sides and neither did Sigrun.

"There's someone else here." Nemain wrinkled her nose and opened her mouth slightly, inhaling deeply. I'd seen her do that before when she was trying to parse scents. I figured it was a cat thing since I'd never seen any of the canines do it, but it seemed rude to ask. "A huldra," she spat.

"There's no need to be rude," a light musical voice said, drawing my attention to the large tree. A tall, slim figure pulled away from the bark of the tree and sauntered towards the dwarves. Like her voice, her movements drew attention, and I found myself unable to look away for a few seconds before the spell broke. I blinked a few times and checked my mental shields but found they were still up.

It's huldra magic, Jinx said quietly in my mind. I was a little alarmed he was able to get around my mental shields, but I shoved that concern away to worry about later. *She's not trying to ensnare you. That was just the passive aspect of her magic. If she tried, you wouldn't be able to take your attention of her as she sank a dagger into your heart. We'll need to practice on your mental shields, little valkyrie.*

I shuddered, and the huldra's watery blue eyes snapped towards me. "Well, what have we here?" She stepped forward, and I avoided looking directly at her eyes, which seemed to help. Her skin was so pale I could see the veins running underneath it. The dark green color reminded me of roots. I blinked when I realized the reason I could see so much of her skin was because she was completely naked. Long, dark brown hair fell to her knees in tangles. Thin branches and vines were wound through it in such a way that I was fairly certain were growing out of her head. She reminded me a little of the nymphs from the fae realm I'd grown up in, but a darkness surrounded her that they never had.

"Like what you see, love?" She purred, twirling some hair around her long, slender finger.

"Not particularly. I like trees, but I've never really had any interest in fucking one."

Nemain barked a laugh, and I heard Damon and Misha do their best to contain their laughter. The huldra's features darkened in anger, giving parts of her skin a bark-like appearance as the texture roughened. I slid a glance towards Elisa and found her staring at the huldra in a very unfriendly manner.

"It's time for you all to leave," Sigrun said flatly. My head snapped towards her, and I barely contained my rebuke. She couldn't possibly mean to just let them go, could she?

"And if we don't want to leave?" the huldra asked, a raspy quality to her voice that hadn't been there before.

"Then we get to play," Nemain said, flicking her wrist so

one of her throwing daggers slid free. Both Mikhail and Magos moved to stand by her side.

"This is a new low for you, Sigrun," the huldra sneered. "You're not even going to fight us? Just let the vampires and whatever that thing is"—she pointed a finger at Nemain—"do all your dirty work? You're not fit to mentor this pretty new valkyrie, and it's a shame you're going to ruin the rest of her life by continuing to think you're still worthy."

"Play time it is," Nemain said, as I started to pull my axe free. My hand froze over my shoulder as Nemain opened a gateway directly behind the huldra. *Oh shit.* She could only open gateways that fast to realms she'd been to frequently, and I doubted she was sending them to a fae or daemon realm. The dwarves moved back, creating more space between themselves and the gateway. But the huldra remained rooted in place, her mouth gaping open as she stared at the gateway and the monsters that crept in the darkness beyond.

Before the huldra could back away, Nemain dove forward and slammed the heel of her hand into the huldra's solar plexus. She flew backwards through the gateway and landed on her ass, tumbling head over heels a few times before coming to a stop. She let out a low growl that was immediately drowned out by dozens of snarls and howls. "I'd run if I were you." Nemain wiggled her fingers, and the huldra whirled around and took off, her long hair streaming behind her. The gateway slammed shut, and Nemain cracked her head from side to side before turning her attention to the dwarves. All but the tall female flinched back. "What should we do with them?"

"Open a gateway back to Svartalfheim," Sigrun said.

"What?" I stared at Sigrun in disbelief. "Don't you want to know why they're here? And why they're working with whoever this seidr practitioner is?"

"I know why they're here and what they're after," she said.

"It's the reason they agreed to work with someone from Vanaheim."

I crossed my arms over my chest and glared at Sigrun. "What are they searching for?"

"The same thing they always are."

Argh.

The dwarves remained silent, glancing back and forth between me and Sigrun. I felt the attention of one of the males with short hair, he was studying me curiously when his green eyes widened. He snapped, and my axe sprang free and flew towards him. He snatched it out of the air and studied it, the other dwarves crowding around him.

"Hey!" I strode towards them. "Give that back!"

The dwarf who had taken my axe looked at the tall female, who must be their leader, and she nodded at him once. He stepped forward and held the axe up horizontally, as if making an offering. Confusion replaced anger, and I slowly reached out. As my fingers brushed the handle, a spark of magic zinged through the wood and several new runes appeared.

"What did you do?"

"It wasn't finished." He shrugged. "I made it a while back. It disappeared after . . . after everything happened."

I lifted the axe. Aside from the new runes, it didn't look or feel any different. At my confused expression, the dwarf sighed. "It will never need sharpening or cleaning. And it would take one hell of a weapon to break it now."

"Oh." I blinked at the axe, running my fingers carefully across the blade's edge. "Thank you?" I said in confusion, not really understanding why he had bothered.

"Don't like leaving things unfinished is all," he said gruffly. "Might have added a few other tricks that you'll just have to figure out on your own."

"Just couldn't leave well enough alone, could you?" The dwarf leader sighed and faced Sigrun. "Our quarrel with you remains the same. We want it back. A new power rising in Vanaheim gave us an opportunity we couldn't refuse, but we are not allied with her. This was a onetime deal. We will go home now."

Sigrun's expression remained one of granite, and I bit back my question about what it was the dwarves wanted. She clearly wasn't going to tell me, at least not now. Nemain stretched out a hand once more, and after a few seconds, a gateway slowly opened, revealing a rocky landscape with a vast city built into a mountainside a short distance away. "No idea if this is where you need to go in your realm, and I don't much care," Nemain said. "Get out."

The dwarven leader eyed Nemain suspiciously. "What are you?"

Nemain bared her teeth. "Fuck around and find out."

The dwarves fled through the gateway, and Nemain snapped it shut.

"It might be for the best if you make yourself scarce for a while," Nemain said to Sigrun. "Find somewhere else to stay."

"No offense, but I'm not staying at your place. It's a bit crowded for my liking."

"Good, because I wasn't offering," Nemain said with a shrug. "Jinx would curse me with bad luck for the rest of my life if I let Viggo stay under the same roof as him."

"Plus, we just got the stench of dog out of the apartment," Mikhail said lightly. "No offense, Gunnar."

If Mikhail was disturbed by the twin glares from the white wolf and Nemain, he didn't show it.

"Fuck," Sigrun swore before stomping off towards her house, Gunnar and Viggo following in her steps.

I spun towards Nemain. "Are you going to tell me what the hell is going on?"

She grimaced. "Not my place to tell you. I'd leave it alone

if I were you. Sigrun will tell you if and when she wants to. It's her problem."

"Well, *her* problem," I growled. "Seems to have taken an interest in *me*. So that kind of makes it my problem too!"

Nemain sighed. "You're not wrong, Bryn. Trust me, I'm not thrilled that a dark practitioner of seidr wants you. But in case you haven't noticed, our darling Sigrun is a wee bit stubborn. I can keep you safe until she pulls her head out of her ass."

I frowned at Sigrun's little cottage, not liking this at all.

"We'll check the workshop and surrounding area. Go check in with Sigrun," Nemain paused. "I'd advise against pushing her on this too much." I watched her walk off towards the workshop, the others following her. Too annoyed to be amused at Nemain being the voice of reason for once.

Elisa remained behind and tucked a loose strand of hair behind my ear. Her black hair shone brightly, falling in a dark wave down her shoulders, and the worried thoughts bouncing around in my head faded. I wondered if the effect she had on me would fade over time. All I could think about was what it would feel like to run my fingers across her jawline before entangling them in that dark hair. "Has anyone ever told you that you look gorgeous in the afternoon sunlight?" I asked and winced at the stupidity. Up until a couple of days ago, Elisa had never been in the sun. Gods, I was such an idiot.

She laughed, her deep blue eyes sparkling with amusement. "I'm glad you were the first person to tell me so." I smiled at her, still feeling like an idiot, but at least she found it entertaining. "You need to go speak with Sigrun."

My smile faded. "I don't know what to say."

"Just be honest."

"And if I can't convince her to stick around and teach me? Or tell me what's really going on?"

"Then we'll find another way." Elisa cupped her hand

against my cheek, and I leaned into her touch, breathing in her scent. The practical side of me knew I was falling for her far too fast, and this could lead to heartache. But I didn't care. Whatever was starting between us felt right. It felt like a part of me I'd been missing all these years had finally fallen into place.

I closed the distance between us and brushed my lips against hers as my fingers dove into her silky hair like they'd been aching to do. Elisa froze for a second, and I smiled against her lips. "Did I finally surprise you?"

Elisa let out a husky laugh and molded her body against mine, kissing me deeply. My body strummed with need, and I almost fell to my knees when I opened my mouth and her tongue slipped into mine. All I could think about was how delicious she tasted and that clever tongue of hers as she dug her fingers into my lower back.

Slowly, we pulled apart, each of us breathing hard. "The kiss was for luck in case you were wondering," I said, my body still taut as a bow string.

"I'll be sure to wish you more luck in the future, then." Elisa kissed me once more and then gently shoved me towards the cottage. "I'll be with the others when you're done."

By the time I reached the front door, I had thought of and dismissed at least half a dozen arguments. I wavered on the threshold. The door was partly open, and I could hear Sigrun moving around inside. Before I could chicken out, I took a deep breath and entered.

The trepidation I'd been feeling was swept away in a wave of anger. Sigrun's home, the refuge she'd built over these years, was destroyed. Every piece of furniture was shattered, the cozy rugs and blankets had been shredded, even the weapons that had hung on the walls were broken. I reached down and picked up the piece of an axe handle that looked like it had been sheared off. The wood wasn't splintered or damaged; it had simply been cut into pieces. I picked up another and saw it was the same. The axe head itself had been broken apart into a dozen pieces, all of equal size.

"Why did they do this?"

"They're looking for something and were pissed about not finding it. The weapons were destroyed by the dwarves," Sigrun said in a monotone voice. "Everything else was likely the huldra. They have very sharp claws that are excellent at shredding."

"I'm so sorry, Sigrun." Not knowing what to do with the broken axe pieces I was holding, I set them down carefully in a pile.

The valkyrie turned away from me and shrugged. "They're just things. They replaced the things that came before them, and now they, too, will be replaced."

"But this is your home. It should be a safe place." I frowned. "It's not safe for you to be here."

Sigrun looked over her shoulder at me, eyes flashing red. "They went through a lot of trouble to lure me away from my home and to be gone before I returned. I am in no danger. They would never attack while I was here."

I wasn't so sure about that. Maybe they would simply come back with greater numbers, but I withheld my comment since it wouldn't help and simply nodded instead. "What were they looking for?"

"Something they didn't find."

My eyes roamed over the mess. I suspected her workshop would be in a similar state, and I was selfishly glad I had picked out my axe and shield. Otherwise, they, too, would have been destroyed.

"Why did the dwarf fix my axe instead of destroying it."

"They don't like destroying things they've made, but they're really angry with me so they made an exception for all of my stuff. But that shield and axe is yours."

I bit my bottom lip as I studied the destruction all around

us. "Are you sure they didn't find whatever it is they're after? They probably created this mess to cover up whatever it is they stole."

"They created this mess because they were pissed off they couldn't find it. They did not find what they were after. I would know if they did." Her tone made it clear she was done with this line of questioning and wouldn't be telling me what they were after. I wondered if Nemain knew, but if she did and hadn't told me yet, she wouldn't tell me now. Nemain kept guarding the secrets of others seriously, and considering all she'd done for me and Finn, I deeply appreciated that about her.

"We could help you get new furnishings," I offered. "Kaysea and Pele have been helping us get furnishings for the apartment that work well with my wings."

Sigrun didn't say anything as she continued to pile up the pieces of broken furniture and weapons. I narrowed my eyes at her. "You're still planning on leaving."

"It's better for everyone."

I bit back my immediate response of "bullshit" and instead picked up the pieces of what I was pretty sure was the blanket Viggo had been sleeping on when we arrived. The skogkatt was being suspiciously quiet where he was curled up next to Gunnar in a corner. They were both watching me, although what they wanted I had no idea.

"What about the dark practitioner who is interested in me?"

"I'll deal with her. Nemain can keep you safe in the meantime." I saw the doubt that flashed in her eyes. Whoever this practitioner was, worried her a lot more than she was saying.

"Or you can teach me how to protect myself," I said. "And we can help you with whatever is going on."

She gave me a humorless smile. "What's been going on has been taking place for centuries. This is nothing new. I'm sorry that you've been drawn into it. That's not what I wanted and it's one of the many reasons I wanted Nemain to keep you away from me."

"Well, I'm involved now. There's no going back." I dumped an armful of fabric onto the pile Sigrun had been building. "I will never choose them, you know. I realize that's one of the reasons you're refusing to mentor me. You think that if I am associated with you in such a way, the other valkyries will turn against me. Your enemies will become my enemies, and I will ruin any chance I have at truly belonging amongst the other valkyries. But you're wrong in thinking that is something I would ever want."

"You're young. I know how you feel now, but we're immortal, Bryn. You will never die of old age, and unless you are struck down, you would be choosing to spend eternity on the outside of your community." Turning away from me, she flexed her hands into fists before releasing them. "You belong with them."

"You're wrong," I repeated, my voice solid and unfaltering. "And it's incredibly arrogant of you to assume what I would eventually want. I've already chosen. I chose Finn." I moved to stand in front of Sigrun. She still had a few inches on me, but I raised my chin and met her unflinching gaze. "I chose Nemain, and while you might have a lot of enemies, I'm pretty sure the devourer-fae-shifter hybrid, who is the daughter of The Erlking and The Morrigan, and has a true talent for pissing people off, has a hell of a lot more enemies than you. She threatened the goddamn Seelie Queen," I said, shaking my head ruefully.

Sigrun grimaced and opened her mouth to argue, but I cut her off. "I choose you, Sigrun. And I will make sure everyone knows it. I'll make sure all the valkyries know it. The Aesir. The Vanir. Everyone in the Yggdrasil realms. So if you don't want to teach me, fine, I can't make you. But know it will change nothing, and I will still be linked with you in the eyes of everyone else."

"This is that goddamn vampire's doing." Sigrun pursed her lips as the muscles of her jaw flexed. "They're all a bunch of scheming assholes."

"I'm a fast learner, and I find myself surrounded by all sorts of beings who can teach me different things. I would like you to be one of them, but I will not force you, Sigrun. I may have chosen you, but you have to choose me as well." I folded my hands in front of me, mimicking the pose I had seen Magos do a dozen times when he was patiently waiting for Nemain to make a decision. I meant every word I had said. Few could claim to be friends with so many different and powerful beings, and I was determined to learn everything they had to teach me. I hoped Sigrun would change her mind and mentor me, but even if she didn't, I would do whatever I could to protect her. Just as I would do for the others. Even though it had only been a few months, our bonds were deep. We were more than friends, we were family.

I hadn't expected to ever belong to a family like this, but now that I had it, I would fight tooth and nail to keep it safe.

As the truth of my new life settled into me, something brushed against my leg. Viggo sat directly in front of me and peered up at Sigrun, no trace of that usual arrogance in his expression. *You will do this.*

"Excuse me?" Sigrun crossed her arms and glared down at the fluffy brown feline. "I don't take orders from you, young one."

I couldn't hide the small smile that played across my lips at a centuries-old skogkatt being referred to as young. Apparently, it wasn't just me and the vamp kids who would always be thought of as children to Sigrun and the other older beings in our group. Viggo might be centuries older than me, but that was nothing to Sigrun who had already seen a thousand years come and go.

What about Gunnar? He agrees with me. The white wolf raised his head and gave a short woof. Sigrun frowned, her arms falling to her sides. *Told you so.*

I looked between the three of them. It was still unclear to me exactly how much they understood of the wolf's thoughts. But if Viggo was on my side, which surprised the hell out of me, I didn't want to derail his efforts.

You've been alone for too long. And despite how amazing I am, and how tolerable the dog is, this forced isolation is getting tiresome. A low growl rippled through the living room, but Viggo only flicked his tail over a few inches. *I've been keeping an eye on the girl since she's been here. She is naïve and a bit daft at times, but genuine about her care for you.* I bristled slightly at his wording but held my tongue. Maybe it was only because I'd met Jinx first, but I found myself preferring the grimalkin's acerbic tone over the skogkatt's. *Besides, she's not bluffing. She'll make clear to everyone her connection to you. So throwing yourself on this metaphorical sword will do nothing. Even if she didn't, that seidr practitioner has an interest in her. She's not going to let it go. Don't you want to know why she has such an interest in Bryn? It seems unlikely she knew the girl would be here, but she immediately recognized what she was and seized the opportunity to speak with her, which means our dear baby valkyrie is in danger. Are you really going to leave her safety up to a mediocre fae cat, that feline mutt and freak of nature, and their motley assortment of vampire pets?*

"You could have left the last bit out," I muttered.

No. No, I don't believe I could have.

Gunnar let out another soft woof, and Sigrun pursed her lips thoughtfully. "I don't remember the last time the two of them ever agreed on anything." Her brown eyes fell on me, and I tried not to get excited at what I thought I saw in them. Acceptance. Begrudging acceptance, but acceptance all the same.

"Does that mean you've changed your mind?"

One side of her mouth tilted up into a small, lopsided smile. "I'll mentor you, Bryn."

Inside, I screamed emphatically and pumped my fist into the air the way I'd seen the vamp kids do when they won a round in whatever video game they were playing. But outwardly, I just smiled widely and kept my tone even. "Thank you, Sigrun. I promise to prove myself worthy of you."

"You already have."

Chapter Fifteen

THE APARTMENT WAS SUSPICIOUSLY quiet when we returned home an hour later. We had helped Sigrun clean up as best we could. The workshop had been in a similar state as the cottage. I didn't understand the hatred between those dwarves and Sigrun. They could be lying, but I believed them when they said they weren't allied with the seidr practitioner. Something else was going on between the dwarves and Sigrun. The weapons that had been crafted by dwarves had been set in a pile and melted into a solid clump that had broken my heart to look at.

Sigrun seemed completely unaffected but the destruction of her workshop. She met it with the same impassiveness as when she'd seen her home. I didn't understand why she wasn't more upset. Instead, she was acting like this was something she deserved and simply accepted. I didn't know what they were after, and Sigrun had shut me down when I'd tried to ask again.

Nemain knew. I was sure of it. But I had about as good of a chance of convincing Isabeau to use her quiet voice for an entire day than I did of getting Nemain to tell me Sigrun's secret.

I was supposed to start training with Sigrun in a few days. Nemain would open the gateway to bring me back to her realm. We'd eventually have to figure out a better schedule or method of me coming and going there, but I was happy that we at least had a start. Sooner or later, I would get the truth from Sigrun about why this seidr dark practitioner was hounding her and interested in me. But at least now I felt like I had time to do so instead of worrying about her simply vanishing.

"Do you think they're downstairs?" I asked as the gateway closed behind me. Finn and I had been staying in the second-floor apartment, which had been vacant before we moved in. Finn spent most of his time in the bottom floor apartment with Isabeau or on the top-floor apartment, only retreating to the second floor when it was time to sleep or if he needed a break from everyone else. He still didn't talk much about his child-hood and what it was like growing up in the prison realm of the exiled fae king and his army of fae devourers.

Luna and another sidhe woman had done their best to protect Finn from the horrors of the realm, but that resulted in him being isolated for most of his life. The noise and chaos of this world overwhelmed him sometimes. It surprised the hell out of all of us that he got along so well with Isabeau, who was rapidly earning the title Lord of Chaos.

Elisa picked up a note that had been left on the counter. I peered over her shoulder and saw Kaysea's beautiful script handwriting. "Kaysea and Zareen took them to Tír fo Thuinn," Elisa said, skimming the rest of the note. "Isabeau wanted to see some fancy cave Kaysea mentioned last week. She says they'll return to her house afterwards and she'll let you know when the kids are ready to be picked up, Nemain."

"Is that safe?" My wings twitched slightly. "Shouldn't we keep Finn out of the fae realms?"

"It'll be fine," Nemain said as she strode over to the couch. As she was about to sit down, Mikhail hopped over the back of the couch and sprawled across the entire thing and closed his eyes. Nemain glared down at him and pulled both her swords free. Mikhail opened one eye at the sound but didn't move as Nemain tossed the swords down on the coffee table. One of the blades dug into the wood, giving the table yet another nick. The throwing daggers landed next to them as Nemain stomped over to an open chair and started unlacing her boots.

Magos sighed and walked over, picking up her discarded weapons and hanging them in their place on the wall next to the door. Out of the corner of my eye, I saw Misha and Damon pillaging the fridge. They looked at me sheepishly and shut the fridge door, arms full of food. "We'll be downstairs enjoying the rare moment of silence in that apartment." Elisa held the front door open for them as they escaped with their bounty.

"It's truly astonishing the amount of food they eat." Nemain shook her head. "To answer your question more fully, it's safe enough for Finn to be in Tír fo Thuinn. The territory of Tír fo Thuinn exists across multiple fae realms, but it belongs to the sea fae. The courts of Unseelie and Seelie have no authority there and only visit it with the permission of the merfolk. I know the cave Kaysea is referring to. It's in a remote location and few beings know about it. They will be fine."

"Okay." I still would have preferred to find Finn safe at home at the apartment, but Nemain was right. Besides, Kaysea would never put Finn in danger, and she was probably the most level-headed person in our group aside from Magos. Once I accepted that Finn would be fine and home soon, exhaustion tugged at me, and I eyed the remaining open chair while I stifled a yawn. It would be difficult to sit in it with my wings and nap, but I wanted to be here when Finn got back.

"I'll let you know when Nemain retrieves Finn," Elisa said, somehow guessing my predicament. "Go rest."

"Aren't you tired too?" I covered my mouth as another yawn escaped me.

Elisa gave me a positively sinful smile, and it suddenly wasn't exhaustion I was feeling. "Why, Bryn? Are you asking me to take a nap with you?"

"Uh. . ." I tried in vain to come up with some type of witty response, but my brain had gone offline at the first hint of that smile.

I can't listen to this, Jinx grumbled.

Nemain huffed a laugh. "Bryn, go nap. Elisa, flirt with the valkyrie later, away from Jinx's delicate sensibilities."

It's bad enough I have to listen to you and Mikhail hate-flirt all the time. I'm not listening to lovestruck teenagers, too.

"Excuse me?" Nemain shot up from where she'd been lounging. Mikhail remained wisely silent, for once not wanting to draw the feline shifter's ire.

I said what I said, Jinx replied haughtily. *I'm going to find Luna.* The black grimalkin trotted to the apartment door, which swung open and shut for him. Nemain glared at the door like she would set it on fire, and I decided it was time to beat a hasty retreat. Just as I approached the door, I decided I couldn't leave quite yet. Spinning on one heel, I strode back to Elisa before I changed my mind.

"Tomorrow night," I blurted out. She arched one dark eyebrow over those exquisite blue eyes, and I clarified my meaning. "Would you like to have dinner with me tomorrow night at The Inferno? You can flirt with me some more because Jinx won't be there, and I'll do my best not to blush from head to toe while you do so."

She smiled wickedly. "It's a date."

Epilogue

THE CRYSTAL clear river snaked its way through the forest, undeterred by the trees that had fallen in the last storm. It persisted, as always. She knew it was foolish to be out there. The treasure the dwarves and huldra had been after was still safe beneath the surface. It frustrated her that the dwarves had teamed up with the seidr practitioner. They should have been smarter than that. The huldra had likely been instructed to kill them if they'd found it. The dwarves despised the Aesir, but that didn't make them friends to the Vanir, who could be every bit as treacherous. The dwarves had learned that lesson long ago, and they would never forget. It was one of the many reasons they'd remained neutral during Ragnarok.

But this particular Vanir knew just what to dangle in front of them to get them to align with her. Gullveig was always good at playing on a person's desires. Sigrun had recognized that voice the moment it spoke in her mind. Like everyone else, she had thought Gullveig was dead, hunted down by the valkyries after Ragnarok. She should have known better.

That bitch always survived.

She would have to tell Nemain and Bryn about Gullveig

and her history with Sigrun and the valkyries. But not today. Gunnar trotted out from the woods like a ghost, his feathery wings tucked in tight. He sat beside her, and she scratched him behind the ears.

"No sign of anyone?" He let out a low-pitched whine and tilted his head, giving her better access. A smile tugged at her lips. "I don't know where I would be without you, my friend."

Viggo had opted to stay behind and was likely curled up in front of the fireplace. The skogkatt was tired from all the spying he'd been doing on Bryn. Truthfully, she was a little annoyed at him for that. The young valkyrie deserved her privacy, but Viggo loved to spy on others and didn't know the meaning of the word boundaries. She'd have to teach Bryn how to detect skogkatts and valkyries who were hiding behind invisibility magic. It was difficult and not foolproof, but it was better than nothing.

Teaching Bryn both excited and terrified her. Before everything had fallen apart, she'd regularly taught the next generation of valkyries, and that was the one thing from her past life she truly missed. But as soon as word got out about Bryn, she would inherit all of Sigrun's enemies. Gullveig clearly wanted something with the young valkyrie. Viggo had recounted the conversation between her and Bryn to Sigrun after the others had left.

"Things have gotten complicated again very fast," Sigrun said with a sigh, causing Gunnar to snort. Knowing she was just stalling, Sigrun raised her hand, palm facing outward. Water erupted as a silver hammer flew out of the river into her hand. The magic of the hammer sparked as it joined with her own, recognizing her at once as its owner. Despite being at the bottom of the creek bed for decades, it looked as perfect as the day it had been forged.

Her throat tightened as she ran her fingers across the runes embedded in the head of the hammer. She knew every one of them by heart. "What does Gullveig want with you?" The hammer remained silent. Its magic might be great, but it was still only a weapon and couldn't answer her. But she remembered the voice of the man who had wielded it once. She couldn't forget that voice any more than she could forget her own name. The hammer belonged to her now, and its magic would respond to no one else. The dwarves wanted it for sentimental reasons, but Gullveig had carved her own mother's still beating heart out of her chest. She understood sentimentality only so she could use it as a weapon against others like she had against the dwarves. No, she wanted it for some other reason, and Sigrun needed to figure out why fast.

"You'll be sticking with me for a while until we figure that out." She swung the hammer in a smooth, practiced motion, and it easily settled into place on her back. The weight felt so different from her favorite axe, but she would get used to it. Pinpricks of energy surged through her as the magic of the hammer flared before settling back down, as if happy to not be hidden away in the river anymore.

"Time to head home, wolf." Sigrun started back down the trail. "We need to eat and rest. Our lives are about to get very interesting again."

Want to Read More?

The next book in the series, A Shift in Ashes is out now! Signed paperbacks with character artwork are available on the Greymalkin Press Shop at www.greymalkinpress.com.

Want to Read a Free Short Story?

Curious about how Nemain and Kaysea met? Want to read other short stories set within the Lost Legacies world? Sign-up for the newsletter at <u>maddoxgreyauthor.com</u> to get free short stories and stay informed of upcoming releases and events!

Acknowledgments

It's still wild to me that this is my fourth published book! Thank you so much for reading *A Shift in Fortune*!

Originally, the plan was to introduce Sigrun in *A Shift in Fate*, but it just didn't work with the overall story and my editor suggested to cut those scenes out. I really didn't want to, so when she suggested turning those scenes into a novella I latched onto that idea. The entire series so far has been from Nemain's POV, and it was really fun to write from someone else's. I hope you enjoyed it! Bryn and Elisa are two of my favorite characters!

If you enjoyed reading this book, it would be incredibly appreciated if you could leave an honest review on Goodreads or whichever platform you prefer. Reviews are super important for authors and we really appreciate it when y'all take the time to leave one! Plus it helps other readers find us :)

Lost Legacies Guide

CHARACTERS:

Bryn - newbie valkyrie; her soul is bonded with Finn's and she is his guardian

Cian - feline shifter with necromantic magic; twin brother of Nemain; has a strained relationship with her but still loves her fiercely

Damon - teenage vampire on the run from the Vampire Council

Dante - necromancer, incredibly powerful and in a long-term relationship with Nemain's brother Cian

Eddie - a dragon who owns and runs a shop of magical oddities and supplies

Elisa - oldest of the teenage vampire runaways

Finn - fae child of the exiled fae king Balor; a prophecy about him says he will bring about the end of the realms

Isabeau - child vampire that the teenage vampires take care of and treat as a younger sister

Jinx - a fae cat known as a grimalkin, him and Nemain have been together since she was born; he's grumpy and has the ability to inflict bad luck on others

Kaysea - mermaid princess and bestie of Nemain; Myrna was her twin sister; older brother Connor is very protective of her

Luna - another grimalkin (because the only thing better than one cat is two cats); unlike Jinx she is sweet and cuddly

Magos - old vampire warrior, his past is a bit of a mystery but he's loyal to Nemain and their relationship is similar to that of a an uncle/niece despite not being related

Mikhail - former vampire assassin of the Vampire Council; nephew of Magos

Misha - part of the teenage vampire group, looks very similar to Elisa but they don't know for sure if they're actually related, either way they consider each other brother & sister

Nemain - feline shifter and fae hybrid with devourer magic; all around freak of nature; raised by Macha and Nevin who she only learned recently were actually her aunt and uncle; biological parents are Badb and Kalen

Pele - daemon who runs the local tavern, The Inferno; close friends with Nemain who she has been in an ongoing casual poly relationship with for centuries

Sigrun - valkyrie, exiled from her people after the events of Ragnarok; has a wolf companion named Gunnar and a magical cat named Viggo

REALMS:

*Note, this is not an extensive list of all the realms because there are many. Only those relevant to the story are mentioned.

Human Realm - the modern world that humans are familiar with; most humans are completely unaware that their realm is one of many or that magical beings walk amongst them

Meenri - the main realm controlled by the daemons after they fled their original home realm

Fae Realms

Mag Ildathach - belongs to the Seelie Court; name means multi-colored plains

Mag Mell - belongs to neither the Seelie or the Unseelie; like all death realms it is difficult to fully comprehend or travel in without necromantic magic; currently where Dante & Cian call home

Tír fo Thuinn - despite being referred to as a realm, this is actually a territory that stretches across all the fae realms, it is the dominion of the sea fae, all the oceans and seas belong to them

Tír na mBeo - only realm shared by the Unseelie & Seelie Queens

Fallen Realms

Kanima - former realm of the feline shifters; this is where Nemain's parents were born; it fell to devourers and the survivors fled to the human realm

Cerulle - former realm of Magos and Mikhail; also fell to devourers; survivors fled to the human realm and were later killed during the vampire and werewolf war

About the Author

After earning a degree in history and political science, Maddox was pulled kicking and screaming from the world of academia and thrust into the tech industry. Because they had bills to pay and nerd muscles to flex.

Whenever possible, they leave reality behind to build fantasy worlds filled with snarky morally grey characters and hot but devious love interests. Maddox currently resides in the northeast, but they'll always consider themselves Californian at heart. They live with their partner and faithful, but often stinky, furry companions.

To get regular email updates about new releases and other announcements, be sure to sign up for the newsletter on maddoxgreyauthor.com

facebook.com/maddoxgrey.author

instagram.com/maddoxgrey.author

tiktok.com/@greymalkinpress